"I'll take

Suddenly Cole couldn't think. Maybe it was all the blood rushing south. He shrugged out of his leather jacket, draped it over Jordan's shoulders and she slipped her arms in. Then he gestured for her to get on his motorcycle. "Where do you live?"

As she settled behind him, she wrapped her arms around his waist and her breasts pressed against his back. "I don't want to go home."

Her words socked him in the gut. "Where to, then?" He held his breath.

"Anywhere. Away from everything. Please." Her arms tightened and one hand roamed over his chest, the other down over his zipper.

His breathing hitched, and as Cole sped onto Las Vegas Boulevard, all he could think about was the heat, and the movement of her plastered to him.

Jordan slid her hand and cupped him through his briefs. And even though she hadn't moved her hand except to accommodate his lengthening, he was the most turned on he'd ever been in his life.

In fact, he felt as if one wrong move and she'd have him begging for mercy....

Dear Reader,

There's nothing sexier than a man in uniform. And there's no place more sizzling than Sin City, Las Vegas. Put the two together and you have a recipe for blazing passion. Eight miles north of the city is Nellis Air Force Base. It's home to the Air Base Defense School, where the Raptors, the elite team of fighter pilots, practice air combat maneuvers in their F-22 jets. These real-life heroes—and heroines—risk their lives every time they take to the skies. They live life on the edge.

But what if a pilot was shot down in combat, injured and permanently grounded? I often think about our men and women who are wounded in the line of duty and how they adjust to life after combat. Maybe he or she will need a challenge of a different sort...hence the premise for my first novel.

I'm so thrilled to be writing for Harlequin Books and hope you enjoy my first Harlequin Blaze novel. If you liked reading about hot desert nights with a fighter pilot—in uniform, and out of it—I'd love to hear from you. Contact me at www.jillianburns.net. And remember, whenever you're betting in Vegas, *Let It Ride!*

Enjoy!

Jillian Burns

Let It Ride

JILLIAN BURNS

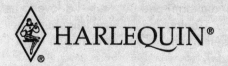

TORONTO • NEW YORK • LONDON
AMSTERDAM • PARIS • SYDNEY • HAMBURG
STOCKHOLM • ATHENS • TOKYO • MILAN • MADRID
PRAGUE • WARSAW • BUDAPEST • AUCKLAND

Recycling programs
for this product may
not exist in your area.

ISBN-13: 978-0-373-79470-6
ISBN-10:   0-373-79470-3

LET IT RIDE

Copyright © 2009 by Juliet L. Burns.

www.eHarlequin.com

Printed in U.S.A.

ABOUT THE AUTHOR

Jillian Burns has always read romance, and spent her teens immersed in the worlds of Jane Eyre and Elizabeth Bennett. She lives in Texas with her husband of twenty years and their three active kids. Jillian likes to think her emotional nature—sometimes referred to as *moodiness*—has found the perfect outlet in writing stories filled with passion and romance. She believes romance novels have the power to change lives with their message of eternal love and hope.

To Wanda Ottewell, for believing in me and sticking by me.

And to Kathryn Lye, for spinning gold from wheat.

And in honor of all America's military heroes in Iraq and Afghanistan who gave their lives or were wounded in the service of their country.

I'd especially like to thank two brave air force personnel for supplying information on fighter pilots and the air force. Thank you to Major Paula Lieberman, ret., and Carrie Hester for being so patient with all my questions!

Any mistakes are entirely my own and not theirs.

1

"TARGET SIGHTED. Three o'clock." Major Cole Jackson nodded toward the amazingly hot blonde across the casino. "The Keno girl with the mile-long legs and the big—"

"Her?" Cole's buddy, McCabe, snorted as he fed another five-dollar bill into a slot machine. "Good luck."

"Why? What's wrong with her?" She was the sexiest thing he'd ever laid eyes on. And after a decade of living on the wild side, that was saying a lot.

McCabe shrugged. "This is Vegas. You got your pick of women."

"Yeah, well, I'll start with her." When Cole had spotted the Keno girl a moment ago the past months of hell had momentarily faded. Having her in his bed for a night or two would certainly help make up for lost time.

Cole's buddies from Nellis Air Force Base had talked him into a week of rest and recreation to celebrate his discharge from the hospital. He was on medical leave until further notice—and who knew how long it would take the powers that be to decide his fate? But for now, he planned to party hard with his buddies and a city full of beautiful women. If he couldn't be in the cockpit of his F-22, this would do.

He stared at the blonde as she moved around the casino, stopping at blackjack and roulette tables. He'd always been a sucker for blondes, and this one had his babe meter clocking in the stratosphere. Her lips alone sent his fantasies to places that could get him court-martialed. His gaze roamed lower to her skimpy red uniform. Damn, what it didn't cover might burn his eyes to the sockets.

"You couldn't even get to two Gs with that one, much less complete a roll. Trust me," McCabe warned.

Ahh! Understanding clicked like an engine turning over in Cole's brain. He shifted on his stool to face his buddy. "She shut you down."

"Him and every other guy who's tried," Captain Alexandria Hughes chimed in from her stool next to McCabe, a satisfied smirk on her face. Their buddy since basic training, Hughes was the kind of chick who'd slug the first guy who tried to treat her like a girly female.

McCabe scowled at her, and then looked back at Cole. "I'm telling you, that Keno girl's got a rep on base as Ms. Crash-and-Bur—" McCabe broke off.

There was a second of awkward silence before Cole jumped in. "Yeah, well, she hasn't seen my maneuvers yet."

"You're full of it, man." McCabe shook his head. "You nail her before my leave is up, and I'll give up women for a month." He raised an arrogant brow as he took a swig of beer.

Son of a bitch. McCabe had just challenged him. A rush of adrenaline coursed through Cole the way it had when he and McCabe and Grady and Hughes had all trained together, pushing the limits of their jets—and their commanders. If this Keno girl was hard to get, all the better. He didn't want some pity fuck. He was ready for something to make him feel alive again. To prove he still had what it took.

And she was it.

"She got a fiancé? Boyfriend?" He'd make sure the playing field was level.

McCabe shrugged. "She was seeing someone—civilian—a while back, but the word is she hasn't used that excuse lately."

"Girlfriend?"

"God, what a waste that would be." McCabe stared wistfully at the blonde, his slot machine forgotten.

Cole couldn't agree more. If he'd ever dreamed of the perfect woman to hit the sheets with, she was it. Long, shapely thighs to cradle his hips and—his gaze went back to her chest—the kind of rack usually only seen in Hugh Hefner's mansion. He stood, his comfortable Levi's suddenly constricting. You were in the hospital too long, Jackson. But thankfully the crash hadn't damaged anything vital to this mission. "All right. You got yourself a bet."

"What?" McCabe's gaze focused on Cole.

"You said you'd give up—"

"I know what the hell I said."

"And she shot you down, right?"

"I prefer to think of it as a failure to pass the pre-flight check. It must be the uniform." With his movie star looks and charm to spare, McCabe was the certified chick magnet of the group. He'd been known to bed two and three women in the same night. Occasionally at the same time.

"She got a rule against Air Force men?" Cole directed his question to Hughes. He wanted some high-level intel on his subject. Of course, he wasn't in uniform tonight....

"I don't know," Hughes answered, her arms crossed over her desert-camo uniform. "And even if I did, I wouldn't tell you."

"Come on, Hughes, you aren't turning all girly on us now, are you?" McCabe grinned at Hughes, but she didn't return his smile.

She stood and finished her beer in one long gulp, then set the bottle down with a thunk. "Poor McCabe. Thirty days without a woman." She leaned in close. "You won't last."

His face screwed up in confusion, McCabe watched Hughes stalk off. "What crawled up her ass?"

Cole shrugged. Air corps or Keno girl, females tended to stick together. Hughes was probably disgusted with him for making the bet. But this Keno girl had a rare kind of beauty that could make a guy forget everything that sucked about his life. Even without the bet, he'd go for her. And after months of surgeries and physical therapy, this challenge put him back into play.

It sure as hell beat sitting around the vet hospital listening to some shrink talk about post-traumatic stress disorder. So, he had a few night sweats and bad dreams. That was to be expected after being shot down and having to make it back to his base camp with a third of his body burned. He'd get over it eventually.

It was his future he was worried about.

All he'd ever wanted to do was be a fighter pilot, and eventually get into the space program. But that wasn't going to happen now. Even if they didn't force a medical discharge down his throat, with this permanent inner ear damage, the best he could hope for was a desk job. Either way, life as he knew it was over.

"So, what do I get if you lose?"

McCabe's voice brought Cole back from his dark thoughts. He grinned at his buddy. "You get to save your right hand a lot of muscle strain over the next thirty days."

"And you risk nothing? Screw that."

"Screw what?" Lieutenant Colonel Grady appeared next to them with his perpetually grim expression. His hulking dark presence tended to scare most dogs and small children.

McCabe explained the challenge, and Grady cut his gaze to the Keno girl. His eyes widened and he whistled under his breath. "Oh, yeah. Ms. Cra—" He cleared his throat. "I'm in. How about that bottle of whiskey Jackson's uncle left him?"

"Damn it, Grady," Cole spoke up, "you've been after my Scotch since we were cadets and you don't even drink. It's fifty-year-old Cragganmore. You know how much it's worth?"

"You want to back out?" McCabe taunted.

"Screw you, McCabe." He could get this girl. He just needed to learn everything about her. "So, if I win, does Grady turn celibate, too?" Cole asked.

"Hey, I nev—" Grady began.

"Hell, no," McCabe cut in. "He's already got the worst temper in Nevada. What he needs is to relax. Learn yoga. Get a massage. There's an old lady on the strip, does that herbal-aromatherapy stuff. I'd give a lot to see him get smeared with sweet-smelling oil and chanting New Age mumbo-jumbo."

Cole grunted at the image. "Hell, I'd bet the whiskey to see that."

"I want that Scotch. You're on." Grady stuck out his right hand to seal the deal and Cole shook it, his insides churning with the dare. He could already taste the sweet flavor of victory. And he couldn't wait to see "Don Juan" McCabe suffer without a woman for a whole freakin' month.

"Here she comes," Grady warned.

A fruity scent teased Cole's nostrils. Dammit, she'd approached him on his deaf side.

He spun to find the Keno girl standing next to him, his gaze drawn to the pale, soft flesh spilling out of her tight, red uniform top. He imagined palming those tits, rubbing his thumbs over the nipples. His body, long denied, roared into four Gs, but he called on years of discipline to focus his attention on her engaging smile and—man, her eyes were such a deep blue they were almost purple.

Up close she was flawless. Her lips moved, but she spoke so softly he couldn't hear her above the rumble and ringing of the slots. He angled his head and leaned closer as he stood and pulled out his wallet.

"—buy a Keno card?" Her voice matched her appearance. Voluptuous and feminine.

"I'll take two." He slipped out a twenty and placed it on her tray.

She handed him the cards and he tossed them on his stool as she dug in her fanny pack for change.

"Keep it." He covered her hand to stop her from making change. Damn, it was like ice. "You're freezing." He curved his fingers around her palm and enclosed her hand in both of his. Soft. Dainty. And so cold.

Her eyes widened, but she pasted on a bright smile as she eased from his grasp. "Thank you." She turned to McCabe and her smile faltered a bit. "Did you want a card, Captain?"

"I think my friend here—" he slapped Cole on the back "—has it covered." He turned to Grady. "You up for some poker?"

Grady nodded and they took their beers and headed deeper into the casino.

The Keno girl's gaze shot back to Cole. "You're a fighter pilot too? A friend of Captain McCabe's?" There was a distinct edge to her voice. What the hell had McCabe done? Or did she have a grudge against all military personnel? Had some airman done her wrong?

He shook his head. "Not if you don't want me to be."

Her smile dropped and she raised a brow. "Don't

lose a friend on my account." She turned to leave, but Cole sidestepped to block her retreat.

"Major Cole Jackson, 81st Airborne. And you are?"

She stared over his shoulder a moment, her lips a tight line. Bringing that gorgeous gaze up to meet his, she put her free hand on her hip. "Jordan Brenner. Mother of five. Looking for a man who can support me and all my kids." Her expression said, *Now will you leave me alone?*

If she had five kids he'd stand on this slot machine and quack like a duck. "Five, huh? What are their names?"

Without missing a beat, she rattled off, "Anna, Billy, Charlie, David and—" she faltered, glanced down at the commercial-grade carpet, then back up at Cole "—Fred!" She smiled triumphantly.

Cole chuckled, unable to keep from returning her mischievous grin. Smiling pulled the scarred flesh on the right side of his face. "Not Eddie? Or Ethan? Or Eugene?"

A hum bubbled up from inside her, and a sweet laugh erupted, but was stifled just as quickly. Something inside Cole stilled. Why would she stop such a wonderful sound?

"All right. You caught me. I couldn't think of an *E* name." She shifted her tray of Keno cards to her other hip and her smile faded.

So did his.

"Aren't you going to fill those out?" She nodded toward the Keno cards on his stool. "They'll be starting another game soon."

He glanced back and scooped them from the stool. "I've never played Keno before. Maybe you could show me?"

Wariness returned to her eyes, but she stepped closer, leaning in to point to his cards as she explained. He inhaled the scent of her fruity shampoo and closed his eyes. Damn. Heat raced up his spine.

"You can pick up to ten numbers on each card. The computer randomly chooses numbers between one and eighty and you win based on how many you matched." She began rattling off the odds of certain numbers being chosen like a calculus professor.

"You really know your stuff."

Her eyes narrowed. "For a blonde? Anyone with half a brain can figure odds if they work here long enough."

So, she had a chip on her shoulder about being labeled a bimbo. He wanted to ask her how long she'd been a Keno girl. She couldn't be much older than twenty-five. But he couldn't open fire on her tonight. He'd do a little recon first.

"Just because you're a beautiful blonde doesn't mean you can't be a genius, too. Look at Jayne Mansfield or Sharon Stone. Both have IQ levels close to Einstein's."

She stared at him, her face inscrutable. But something flickered briefly in her eyes and hit him right in the gut. As he stared back, the air between them vibrated as if he'd just started up the jets of his Raptor.

But he didn't want to come on too strong too soon, so he broke eye contact, severing the connection. "I'll let you get on with your work."

She stepped away and fidgeted. "Enjoy the casino, Major."

Cole watched her leave, enthralled with the way her

perfect little butt moved beneath the miniskirt. A shock wave of lust roared through his blood straight to his dick and he tightened his jaw. Yeah, he needed to get control.

He'd made first contact. This time tomorrow, he'd have an intelligence report to aid him. Getting her into bed within a week? That was a challenge he was more than ripe for even without the added bonus of winning the bet.

JORDAN TRUDGED into the female employees' room, tossed her tray in a bin and kicked off her heels. She was bone-tired, and her feet were killing her. Praying Mom had had a good afternoon and evening, Jordan snatched her time card and punched out. How long before Mom got to be too much for Mrs. Simco to handle?

"TGIF." Sherri groaned as she rubbed her feet.

"Don't you have to work tomorrow?" Jordan did, but at least she didn't have classes in the morning, only her regular shift tomorrow night. She and Mom spent Saturday mornings at the Laundromat.

"Umm-hmm, but somehow, saying 'Thank God it's Monday' just doesn't have the same kick." Sherri grinned and peeled off her costume.

"True." Jordan smiled.

"Besides, Friday means the kid is with his dad and Toby is picking me up. You want a ride, hon?" Sherri's son was ten, but was already acting the rebellious teen. Toby was a bartender at the Luxor hotel and casino and got off work at the same time as Sherri.

"And where would I sit in his Miata? Besides, my apartment is totally out of your way."

"I saw you talking to that tall, dark and dangerous guy with Captain McCabe…"

Oh, no. Here it comes. The you-need-to-get-laid speech.

"Which one? They all start looking alike after so many years."

But she was lying. There'd been something about the scarred major that had lingered in her mind as she'd wandered the casino selling her cards. Something compelling that had nothing to do with his thick brown hair, or the subtle defensiveness in his bearing. It wasn't even the scars running down the side of his neck and right hand. It was something in his eyes.

"You're kidding, right?" Sherri threw her an incredulous look. "Dark hair, bomber jacket, fresh scars down the right side of his neck? Don't you want to see if he's got scars anywhere else?"

"He's just like all the rest, Sherri." No different than a thousand other hotshot flyboys roaming around The Grand.

Except…he'd made that comment about intelligence and beauty. And he'd made her laugh. She couldn't remember the last time she'd laughed out loud. And, most of all, he'd ended the encounter without propositioning her.

Stop with the fairy tale, Jordan. That's what had gotten her into the mess her life had become in the first place.

Sherri scowled. "Are you still pining over Mr. Banker-dude?"

"After I caught him with that showgirl? No way!"

"So, forget about waiting for a commitment right

now. Just have a wild fling. You don't have to be in a relationship to get you some, girl. You need a man."

Irritation overtook Jordan. Her friend had it wrong. She didn't need anyone. She'd never depend on a man again. She'd run off with bad-boy-Ian and been deserted. And she'd dated safe-guy-Bob and been cheated on. It may have taken only two failed relationships, but she'd finally learned men weren't reliable. She reined in her annoyance. Sherri was a good friend. She meant well. She'd helped Jordan a lot when she'd first started working here six years ago, teaching her how to earn bigger tips by smiling and flirting, and helping her evade the advances of the worst drunks.

"I know you're thinking of my best interests, Sherri, but all I need is to ace my finals next week. And getting involved with some flyboy from Nellis will not help me memorize differential equations."

"Oh, I don't know. I always did better on a test if I had a good screw the night before. Helped me relax."

"Sherri!" Jordan managed not to roll her eyes.

"All I'm sayin' is, that was one fine piece of man-meat staring at you tonight like you rocked his world. Just think about it if you see him again."

Think about it? Hadn't she just been convincing herself *not* to think about him?

After she changed clothes she left through the hotel's employees' entrance, heading for the bus stop past the parking garage behind the hotel. Even at two in the morning, Vegas vibrated with noisy traffic and tourists.

But she'd long grown tired of the bright flashing lights she'd once found so exciting.

She glanced down the street toward the bus stop and spotted the bus already there. Jordan dodged a few cabs and a limo as she sprinted across the street. "Wait!" She waved her arm just as the bus pulled away in a wheezing cloud of exhaust.

"Crap!" It'd be twenty minutes before the next bus came by. She stuck her fists inside her denim jacket pockets and shifted her weight from sneaker to sneaker. Her body screamed for a hot bath and a soft bed, so she closed her eyes and envisioned the day she earned her programming degree. Once she did, her life would change.

She'd get a respectable job with a decent salary. Buy a home of her own with two bedrooms so she wouldn't have to sleep on the couch. Have professional care for her mom. All she had to do was stay smart, stay focused.

Not let some Casanova derail her plans. Again.

But every once in a while her heart just wanted to let loose all the wild feelings inside. Toss the laundry basket and run screaming into the night.

"Hey." A strong hand gripped her arm and Jordan jumped. "Got a dollar?"

She let out a relieved breath as she recognized one of the bums that slept in the alley behind the hotel. She could smell the alcohol on his breath. But booze wasn't the worst odor. Poor old guy. But for the grace of God…

A motorcycle engine revved and tires screeched. "Let go of the lady," a deep voice ordered from behind her.

The old man yanked his hand away and backed off. Jordan spun around.

The Air Force major. He sat astride a monstrous black motorcycle, his gaze focused menacingly on the old man. His tight, low-riding jeans and black leather jacket personified danger as he curled his fists around the handlebars.

Her body sizzled as she stared at him. The image burned into her psyche, drawing her into the fantasy of the rugged loner coming to her rescue, sweeping her into his arms and—

"I'm fine, Major," she blurted out to stop her crazy dream. She unzipped her backpack and dug around for one of the prepaid cards she'd bought. One of the diners close to her apartment had a program for the homeless. A way to ensure a handout didn't go to buy booze. "This will get you a hot meal and coffee at Zelda's Café on fifty-fourth." She handed the old man the card, and he snatched it from her and took off.

From the corner of her eye she saw the major get off the bike and move toward her.

"You shouldn't encourage those people."

She turned. "He's harmless."

He rubbed his jaw and took a step toward her.

Her chest tightened as he came closer. Her insides coiled with a tension she'd been trying to deny since his comment about blond geniuses. She knew it was just a pickup line, and she'd heard better. But he'd said it as if he really believed it.

"That happen often?"

She shook her head. "No. At least, not in a while."

His dark eyes searched her body, his gaze moving down from her breasts to her legs and up again.

Her stomach clenched with a sharp ache. It'd been too long since she'd had sex, that's all. Why had she waited? Oh, yeah. The whole trying-not-to-make-the-same-mistake-twice thing. She'd told Bob she wanted to wait until they were really committed, and he'd agreed. Too easily, she could see now. And it'd been easy for her, too. Easy and safe.

She'd never felt the kind of ache for Banker Bob that she did tonight for the Air Force major.

"He'll probably trade the card for booze or dope," he said.

Straightening her shoulders, she bristled. "Well, I have to try." His subtle musky cologne drifted to her on the breeze and she drew in a long, slow breath.

He looked down the street, then back at her. "I could give you a ride."

She studied his black bike. Almost a quarter of a century old and she'd never ridden on a motorcycle. An image invaded her mind of riding behind him, her cheek pressed against his back and her palms clutching his hard abs. The vise in her chest squeezed with a danger-ous desire.

"Hey, I understand." The major headed for his bike and swung his leg over the seat. He looked at her as he rolled the bike forward and the kickstand lifted. "You don't know me." His jaw muscle clenched as he turned the key and started the engine. The bike roared to life and he set his boot on the steel footrest and looked up at her. "Yet." Without another word he curled his fists and took off out of the parking lot.

A panicky sense of lost opportunity swept over her. Something inside her wanted to run after him and yell at him to come back, that she'd changed her mind. It was her gnawing inner voice begging for a night of reckless abandon. How could she feel so out of control? How could she even consider it?

Then the bike made a U-turn down the street and roared back into the nightclub parking lot behind her. The engine shut off, and he shoved the kickstand down and strode toward her. She watched the sway of his hips, the tight fit of his T-shirt beneath the jacket, the set of his jaw.

"Decided I'd wait with you until the bus comes."

Jordan tried to swallow past the hard lump in her throat. Even security-conscious Banker Bob had never been willing to lose sleep to make sure she got home okay. "Thank you."

He nodded, but didn't speak, just stood next to her with his arms crossed over his chest.

His leather-mixed-with-man scent tantalized her. The coil in her tightened more, her muscles tensed and she couldn't even look at him.

You're an idiot, Jordan Brenner. So, he was sexy. So were a thousand other players trolling the casino looking to get laid. He just had a different approach. She should remember this guy was a friend of Captain McCabe's, the most prolific serial dater in Nevada. And, she wasn't a naive eighteen-year-old anymore, a girl who ran off with the first guy to charm her jeans off. She had responsibilities. She didn't get swept off her feet.

When the bus pulled up, she climbed aboard without a backward glance.

2

"JORDAN ELIZABETH, this underwear is indecent!" Tammy Brenner hissed as she held up a pair of thong panties.

Snatching them from her mom's fingers, Jordan sighed. "They're for work, Mom. So they don't show under the uniform, remember?"

"I don't like you working in that place," Tammy said. "Showing off everything God gave you."

At least today Mom remembered where Jordan worked. "It won't be for much longer. Soon, I'll have my degree." She stuffed the rest of their underwear and bras into a clean trash bag and carried the empty laundry basket over to the buzzing dryer. "Then I'll start applying for a better job." Her stomach clenched at the thought. A part of her was so ready to get away from casino work. Another was scared to death. What if she failed her finals? Or what if all the corporate honchos took one look at her and decided she wasn't qualified? She needed to buy an ultra-conservative business suit. And maybe darken her hair…

The boom of jet engines scraped across the sky as the Thunderbirds' buzzed over the city, practicing maneuvers. Car alarms went off outside the Laundromat and her mother started screaming.

"What is that? What's happening?" Tammy's voice escalated and started to quiver.

Jordan rushed over and put her arm around her mom. "It's only the jets from the air base, Mom, remember?"

"I want to go home. My regulars at the diner will miss me."

Oh, no. She'd been doing so well this morning.

"But I need you here with me. We make a great team, don't we?"

When her mom didn't answer, Jordan gave up and stuffed the last of the towels from the dryer into the basket. She knew from experience she better get her mom home as soon as possible. Sticking the basket under her arm, she snatched up the trash sack of clean clothes, and led her mom by the arm out of the Laundromat.

"No. I want to go back to my house. I hate this place!" Tammy jerked out of her hold and stopped on the already scorching sidewalk, glaring at Jordan as if the illness was all her fault.

And maybe it was. If she hadn't quarreled with her mom and run off to Vegas with Ian, maybe her mom wouldn't have had the breakdown and been fired. No. The two incidents were years apart. Not related. She refused to start another self-destructive spiral of blame. Mom had Alzheimer's. A medical condition that had nothing to do with a teenage daughter's stupid mistake.

"Let's go home, Mom. We can watch *Sleepless in*

Seattle again before I go to work, okay? Would you like that?" She tried to lead her mom gently toward the bus stop, speaking soothingly about visiting Mrs. Simco and seeing her new fish. Mom loved watching Mrs. S's aquarium. But when the bus pulled up, and she tried to get her mother to climb the steep metal steps, Tammy wouldn't budge.

"No!" She stuck her bottom lip out like a toddler and shook her head, refusing to move.

Jordan shifted the basket of towels higher on her hip and put her arm around her mom's shoulders. "It's okay. You like riding the bus."

"I want to go home," Tammy wailed. She twisted out of Jordan's grasp and headed at a brisk walk down the sidewalk.

"Mom!" Jordan dropped the clean clothes and went after her. Her mother shouted and cried for someone to help her as Jordan tried to reason with her.

Several people were staring, but that was the least of her worries. The last time Tammy had been this bad, it had taken a trip to the doctor's office and a sedative to calm her down. Just getting her to the doctor had been a nightmare involving a 911 call.

The knowledge that her mother would require a special facility soon broke Jordan's heart.

One day at a time. The saying had become her mantra. Sometimes it was the only thing that held the panic at bay and allowed her to keep going.

"Look, Mama." Jordan pointed at the convenience store beside them. "They have slurpies. Can I have one?" Asking for her mom's permission was an inspired tactic. Soon, Tammy had bought her little girl her favorite childhood treat and was happily back at the bus stop with their clean clothes, which by some miracle were still sitting where Jordan had dropped them. Crisis averted.

For today.

A LOUD BANGING jerked Cole off the bed into a crouch, his right hand scrambling for his weapon. It took a moment for desert terrain to fade and the lush hotel room to come into focus. His breath came in short, heavy spurts. He wasn't in hostile territory, covered in sand and blood, making his painful way back to base.

Snapping his wrist up, he checked the time, wiped his temple on his shoulder, and stood. Eighteen hundred hours. Six o'clock. In the evening.

The hotel door banged again. McCabe yelled, "Jackson, you in there?"

Cole scrubbed his face and ran a hand through his hair, then moved to let his buddy in. "Geez, McCabe, what the hell's with all the pounding?" Not waiting for an answer, he turned and headed for the john, leaving McCabe to make himself at home.

When he returned, McCabe was slouched in a corner wing chair, boots propped on the writing desk.

"You could have just called my cell," Cole said, rummaging through his duffel.

"I did."

Damn. Cole hadn't heard his cell ring. He still hadn't

adjusted to not being a hundred percent. Like he wasn't a whole man.

Maybe it was true.

"You look like crap, buddy. You been asleep all day?" McCabe asked.

"I'm on vacation." After seeing Jordan safely on the bus, he'd come back to his room, but he hadn't slept much. He'd had the nightmare again and then he'd lain awake thinking about his last mission, going over in his head what he could have done differently. If he hadn't been such a damn hotshot.

Avoiding his thoughts, he'd headed for the Centrifuge downstairs—God love Vegas's twenty-four-hour casinos—and nursed a couple of tequilas until soaps came on the television behind the bar. But he wasn't about to admit any of this to McCabe.

McCabe leaned back and clasped his hands behind his head. "I got us tickets to the Bullring at the Motor Speedway tonight," McCabe said. "Thought we'd head over to the all-you-can-eat lobster at the Mandalay first. Grady and Hughes are waiting downstairs."

The thought of seafood made his stomach heave. "You guys go on." He shot his buddy a cocky grin. "I've got a bet to win." No way he could hold his head up around McCabe if he lost this wager. They'd been competitors since their first day of flight training.

McCabe shot off the chair. "Are you kidding me? These are front-row seats to Legends Cars. They got Thunder Roadsters, man. That Keno girl won't end her shift until 2:00 a.m. You got plenty of time."

He didn't know which irritated him more. That McCabe called her 'that Keno girl,' or that he knew when her shift ended. "Her name's Jordan."

"Who?"

"The blonde from last night. Jordan Brenner." He smiled remembering the way she'd introduced herself. "Mother of five."

"What? She's got kids?"

He looked at McCabe. "No, she— Never mind."

"You okay, buddy?"

"I'm good. Thanks for the ticket, but I'm flying solo tonight."

Cole headed to the bathroom, lathered up some shaving cream, and smeared it over his jaw.

"So, you're going to sit around in the casino for eight hours and watch her work?"

"Watching a woman like that beats watching souped-up roadsters race around a track hands-down."

"Fine. But it won't make any difference with her."

Cole shot McCabe a parting hand gesture and then finished shaving, his thoughts centered on Jordan. His pulse revved up as he yanked the tags off a new shirt. Just thinking about her dusted all the morbid cobwebs from his mind.

With the thrill of the challenge coursing through his veins, and the thought of getting that gorgeous body beneath his, he went down to the casino.

"This is all your fault, McCabe." Hughes scowled at him, and then took a huge bite out of her hot dog.

Captain Mitch McCabe scooted along the hard metal bleacher and picked up a nacho. The Speedway was crowded tonight, the roadsters were amazing, and the hot dogs and beers were only a dollar. What was not to love? "What'd I do now?" He had to raise his voice over the roar of the stock cars revving up at the starting line.

"Making that bet with Jackson. Is nothing sacred? The man's been in the hospital for two months, for Pete's sake."

"Why is it always for Pete's sake? What's Pete got that I don't?"

Hughes glared at him and punched his arm.

"Ow!" He rubbed his arm. Good ol' Hughes never had qualms about telling a person exactly how she felt. That's what he liked about her. He gestured to Grady on his other side, sipping a bottle of water. "He was in on it, too. Why is it my fault?" Mitch blamed himself for a lot of things, but not the bet last night.

"You're the one who challenged him to go after that poor girl. How do you think she would feel if she knew he was just trying to win a bet?"

"First of all—" Mitch swallowed a chip dripping with gooey cheese "—poor girl? The woman can take care of herself. She sure as hell shut me down."

"And that's why you really did this, isn't it?" Hughes just wouldn't let it go. "You're infuriated that some woman actually turned you down."

"Second—" he planned on ignoring that remark "—Jackson needed a challenge. Trust me, this is just the thing to take his mind off his situation."

Grady grunted. "Permanently grounded." He shook his head. "But the Air Force has reassigned pilots before."

"If they don't discharge him," Hughes said.

"Did Jackson mention a reassignment request?" Mitch kind of hoped Jackson might get assigned here at Nellis.

Grady shook his head. "Not to me. And it could take weeks for his commanding officer to get the paperwork in order one way or the other. He's just gonna have to wait it out. You know how it is. Hurry up and wait."

When Mitch had first heard Jackson had been shot down and was MIA, guilt and worry had kept his insides churning. Then they'd heard Jackson had wandered into the Iraqi base camp after two days in the desert, looking more dead than alive. And he hadn't looked much better when Mitch had visited him in Maryland at the hospital at Andrews AFB.

The memory burned like acid in his stomach. He should have been there, with his buddy, in Iraq, watching his back. And he would have been if he hadn't made an ass of himself over Luanne.

Mitch's hand hurt and he looked down. He opened his clenched fist and stretched the fingers until he could feel them again. The track came into focus and he realized he'd missed the first two laps of the race thinking about those dark days of his divorce.

He glanced over at Hughes and something eased inside him. She was leaning forward, elbows on knees, watching the race the same way she did everything: with intense interest. Her ball cap was turned backward, as usual. Her cheeks were bulging with the last of her hot dog, and she had a glob of mustard on the corner of her mouth.

He grinned, glad she was back after two years stationed at Langley. She was the kind of pal who stuck by you through hell and back and always told it like it was. He never had to guess what she was thinking and she never ever lied to him.

Either she was involved in watching the race, or she didn't want to yell over the noise, but he knew she hadn't dropped the subject.

And sure enough, as the tow trucks cleared the track of a messy crash, she turned to him. "It was a stupid thing to do, McCabe. Jackson may like the challenge, but what if that girl turns him down? Have you thought about how it might affect him? He'll be worse off than before. And minus his treasured bottle of Scotch."

Mitch shrugged. "We've always competed, always dared each other. And you know he wouldn't want to be treated any different just because he's been injured."

Hughes stared at him with pursed lips, and then looked down at the beer she held between her legs. "I guess you're right."

It struck him suddenly that Hughes had changed since being at Langley. Something was different. He wondered if something had happened. Well, if she wanted to talk about it, she'd bring it up. "Hey, how about we hit Duffy's after this? See if we can get lucky tonight." He grinned at her.

The look she gave him was…weird. Like she pitied him or something. Yeah—even though they'd kept in touch, sending text messages and e-mails—Hughes was different. Used to be she'd flip him off after falling for his latest practical joke. Then she'd shoot him an evil grin and plot her revenge.

But lately, she just seemed testy.

First, Jackson's risk of being discharged. Now, whatever was bugging Hughes… These guys were the only buddies he had. Mitch felt his world was changing. And damn, he hated change.

COLE HAD CONVINCED himself Jordan couldn't be as beautiful as he'd remembered.

But she was.

Seeing her tonight hit him hard all over again. He watched her for a half hour, studying her smile and gestures, the swing of her butt and the sensuous shift of her breasts when she moved. She looked at him a couple of times, meeting him stare for stare. He considered smiling and waving, but the mood didn't seem to warrant it. Her mouth would tighten and she'd break eye contact.

His mission tonight was to make discreet inquiries of her coworkers. He hit pay dirt with a redheaded Keno girl who seemed to relish playing matchmaker.

He learned Jordan had worked at The Grand almost six years and that she attended the University of Nevada at Las Vegas weekday mornings. The redhead said she'd been seeing a banker several months ago, but no one since. Cole already knew she had a soft spot for homeless bums. And one other thing he'd picked up last night: when he'd told her he'd wait with her until her bus came, the look on her face had left him...aroused.

Unfortunately, tonight that shocked and vulnerable look was nowhere to be seen. As soon as Jordan spotted him waiting for her in the parking lot behind the bus stop, she called out to him.

"I don't need a bodyguard, Major. Really, it's fine."

Cole raised a brow, shoved the kickstand down and got off his Harley. "Maybe." He closed the distance between them. "Maybe not."

Damned if she didn't look sexier in her civilian clothes. Her teased hair and showgirl makeup seemed out of place with the faded jeans, denim jacket and worn sneakers.

She crinkled her brow, and then checked the street. "I wait here every night. I'm perfectly safe."

"Would anyone stop to help if you got mugged?" He grunted. "Maybe, maybe not."

A withering sigh escaped her as she turned back to stare at him. "So, is this what you do? Ride around all night patrolling the strip looking for damsels in distress?"

"Used to patrol the Baghdad strip, does that count?" A smile tugged one side of his mouth. "Look. Maybe we could just talk until your bus gets here."

"At two in the morning, you want to have a stimulating conversation about...?"

"About you."

"Why?"

"You interest me. Is that so hard to believe?" Unbelievably, it was true. She was fascinating. He wanted to know everything about her.

"Yes." She glanced along the street again, as if willing the bus to hurry. Damn, that was rough on a guy's ego.

"You think you know me, or my type." It wasn't a question, but he wanted to see what she'd say. He stepped closer, and she instinctively took a step back. He cocked his head. "Are you afraid of me?"

"No. I just don't trust you."

He didn't blame her. "Fair enough. In your line of work, you've probably dealt with your share of jerks. You think I'm only after sex?" Wasn't he?

"Aren't you?"

"I could get that anywhere in this town."

"Then go for it."

The challenge flamed in his chest. "I don't want anyone else."

"So, you admit you want to get laid."

He blinked. She was no shrinking violet, was she? But there was no reason not to be honest with each other. "What red-blooded man doesn't?" he said with a shrug. "I never claimed to be celibate." He folded his arms. "Look, I won't deny the minute I saw you, I was attracted to you. And it'd be great if we got together. But you're…interesting. I haven't asked you up to my hotel room, or tried to put my hands all over you. I just thought I'd get to know you."

She frowned, and something about the look in her eyes made him think she might be wavering.

"Here's the deal," he said. "You ask me something about me, and then I get to ask you a question."

"You assume I want to know you."

"Fine. We'll stand here avoiding each other in awkward silence until your bus comes."

She surprised him by letting out a frustrated half growl, half groan. "All right, Major. You've seen combat?"

"Call me Cole. And yeah. Served one tour in Afghanistan and two in Iraq."

"And you're going back when your leave is over?"

Back into combat? Not likely. The thought of a desk job, or—even worse—a medical discharge, made his throat close up. And knowing he'd never fly again was a physical pain in his chest. But he couldn't talk about it.

"My turn." He studied her intensely for a second. What did he most want to know? "What's your favorite time of day?"

She looked puzzled. Good. He'd caught her off guard. "Early mornings." She cleared her throat. "Your injuries." She gestured toward his neck. "Were you… shot down?"

He kept his features blank as he nodded, then smiled and stepped closer, wanting to catch a whiff of her unique scent. "Yoga at sunrise and herbal tea, am I right?"

She shook her head and barely stopped a smile. "Pilates and diet cola. At nine. Did you get a Purple Heart?"

He grimaced. "Not yet." And he wasn't likely to since he'd disobeyed orders. "What's your favorite dessert?"

"Now why," she frowned, "would you waste one of your questions on something like that?"

"We didn't put a limit on questions."

"Hmm. Maybe we should have."

In answer he merely raised a brow.

Then she actually, finally, smiled. "Okay, okay. Ben and Jerry's Oatmeal Cookie Chunk."

Man, she was beautiful. And real, somehow.

"Let's see…" She put her finger to her lips and studied him from head to toe. "Any brothers and sisters?"

He nodded. "Two of each."

"Wow. Four siblings? I always wanted a brother or a sister."

"Believe me." He moaned and shook his head, recalling all the torment he'd lived through as the youngest of five. "Count your blessings. Five kids. One bathroom. You're the math whiz. What were my odds?"

She laughed and something eased inside him.

"You're calling me a math whiz? I know what kind of intelligence it takes to become a fighter pilot."

Taking a half step toward her, he reached out with one finger and touched her cheek. "You have a beautiful laugh."

Her smile dropped, but she didn't push his hand away. If he moved one millimeter closer, her nipples would brush his leather jacket. She licked her lips and he couldn't stop a raspy sound from escaping his throat as he caught the action. What could she do to him with those lips?

"Whose turn is it for a question?" she asked quietly.

His mouth hovered above hers. Had she leaned toward him? He lowered his head a fraction more. "Mmm. Mine." His lips brushed the corner of her mouth. "When's your next day off?" he mumbled against her cheek, then nuzzled along her jaw.

"Tuesday." Her voice sounded breathy and she softened against him. His cock swelled in his jeans.

His finger glided up her throat and lifted her chin. Just as their lips touched, the bus gasped to a stop beside them. She jerked her head back and stepped away.

But this time, after she found a seat, Cole caught her glancing back at him with a disturbed expression.

He ran a hand through his hair, and then turned toward his bike. He sure as hell didn't want to head to the hotel yet. It wasn't as if he'd sleep anyway. He was still as hard as stone.

He'd been so close. So close to tasting her. To feeling her in his arms. And he hadn't even planned that move. He needed more sleep. And sex. Ten months in Iraq. Three in the hospital. Geez, it'd been more than a year since he'd spread a woman's thighs and lain between them. Felt them wrap around him as he pushed into her.

Into Jordan. He couldn't picture any other woman in his bed right now. He closed his eyes as he remembered the softness of her cheek. The chase made him feel alive again, but so did the woman herself. And he only had five more days to seduce her if he wanted to win that bet with McCabe.

3

SUNDAY NIGHT Jordan headed for the break room, dreaming not of slipping out of her heels and getting off her feet for a half hour, but of the feel of Cole's lips brushing hers.

She'd been playing with fire by giving in to his suggestion last night, and she'd come close to letting him burn her resolve to a crisp. His hard body had fitted so rightly against hers, and his touch had sizzled along her skin.

She stopped in her tracks when she walked into Cole pacing by the break-room door clutching a paper bag. Her world filled with the fragrance of heated musky aftershave and old leather.

Oh, no. Her resistance was already weak. She didn't know if she could fight her feelings tonight. It felt as if the coil inside her chest would snap at any moment. If only there was such a thing as an inoculation against sexual attraction.

She stepped back and flattened the empty tray against her chest like a shield. "Are you stalking me, Major?"

He gave her a skeptical look. "It's Cole. And do

stalkers usually bring their victims Oatmeal Cookie Chunk?" He held out the paper sack.

"What?" She set the tray on a nearby stool, then cautiously took the bag and peered inside. "It really is—" She looked up at him. "But where did you—" She stared into the bag again. How in the world... They only have this flavor at Christmas. How'd you find it in May?"

He grinned. "I'm a man of many talents."

"I bet." She didn't try to hide the sarcasm in her tone. "Look, I'm not—" Oh man, she couldn't be that rude. Dropping her gaze to the floor, she stalled by shifting her weight from foot to foot before looking up at him. "Thank you for the thought, but—" she shoved the bag against his chest "—I have to go." She twisted away.

"Jordan."

She stopped, but didn't turn back.

"It's just ice cream."

For the first time she doubted her instincts. Was she being too cynical? Had she let the world change her into one of those bitter man-haters? Rather, experience had taught her a few valuable lessons. There was a difference between bitterness and discretion.

She spun on her heels and pinned him with an accusing eye. "You're wasting my time, and yours, Major. I'm not interested."

He scowled, his brows lowered to create a deep crease. Tossing the ice cream on the stool with the tray, he closed the distance between them, seized her shoulders, and lowered his head to take her lips.

Jordan stiffened at first, trying to fight the rush of

heat assailing her, but his lips were so persuasive, so thorough in their lush assault, she quickly surrendered. The taste of him flooded her senses as he slid in just a touch of his tongue. Recklessly, she deepened the kiss, pressing her body to his. Her arms snaked around his neck, and her fingers curled into his thick hair.

No. She wouldn't give in. She couldn't allow herself to be ruled by her impulses again. She pulled away. "Stop."

He dropped his hands from her back, his breathing deep and ragged. "I want you, Jordan. I'm only in Vegas for a week. I don't know where I'll end up after that. For me, there's only now. And all I know is, I want you. No promises. No strings. No games."

She searched his face, staring at him for any sign of duplicity. But all she could see in his deep-brown eyes was need. Intense and unvarnished.

Finally, she looked away. "I appreciate your honesty, Cole. But I'm not good at that kind of thing." She brushed past him and darted into the break room.

THE FLUORESCENT LIGHTS cast a jaundiced glow as Jordan wound her way through the casino after her break. The rumble and beeping of slot machines echoed the feeling in her chest. Agitated. On edge. She was either the smartest single woman on the planet or the stupidest person to ever sell Keno cards. She caught herself searching the casino for the major, but he was gone.

The same frantic regret from the other night filled her. His kiss had burned all the way down her body. Why had she told him no? What was she saving herself for?

She'd been careful for so long, trying not to repeat her mistakes. But choosing a man she thought was a nice guy hadn't worked out, either. Banker Bob had still dumped her for a showgirl. So, why not have a fling with some guy who at least admitted he only wanted a one-time deal?

She'd assumed he'd been stationed at Nellis. But he'd said he was only in Vegas for a week. Maybe he was returning to combat? Maybe he wouldn't make it back next time. The last thought made her chest hurt.

She was almost due to clock out. All she had to do was make it through tomorrow, then she'd be off work for two days. But, she had to spend every free moment studying. Even tonight when she got home. Failing was not an option. As she strolled around the slots, her headache sharpened, shooting down to the base of her skull.

She needed a clone. Just for this week. Just until she could get her degree. She dreaded going home and dealing with Mom. And what kind of ungrateful daughter did that make her? All her life her mother had been there for her. No matter what. She used to say, "You and me against the world, kiddo. We'll make it as long as we stick together." And she'd been right.

But it was Cole's words that played in her head like a looped movie trailer...*all I know is, I want you.* The raspy hunger in his voice made her breathing hitch.

She missed sex. She bit her lip at how she'd almost told him she wanted him, too. To take her to his hotel room. Or his apartment on base, or whatever. Wherever. Anywhere. As long as he threw her on the bed and they went at it like horny teens. Just for a few wild, reckless hours.

Sherri was right. A hot bout of sex would release the stress and help her study. Sex didn't always have to be about love and commitment. Sex was really just about sex. The tension inside her stretched so taut she'd snap if she didn't relieve some of the pressure.

"Well, hi there, pretty thang," a tall youngish guy grabbed her bottom.

She knocked his hand away. "Get lost!" She couldn't take it anymore. Was this what she had to look forward to for the rest of her life if she flunked her finals?

"Jordan!" her boss came up behind her, soothing the guy with a card for a complimentary dinner before he took her arm and urged her toward the break room. "You know how it works. If someone gets handsy, call security. You never, ever yell at the customers. Now, clock out. Go home." He gave her a serious glare. "Don't ever let that happen again."

Oh, my gosh. What had she done? She needed this job. And she'd been a model employee for years. Working double shifts, and filling in for absent or late co-workers. He wouldn't fire her for this one infraction, would he?

A crazy rebellion boiled to the surface. So what if he did? Hadn't she already been deserted in this unfamiliar city without a job? She'd survive somehow. Without even bothering to change, she threw her backpack over one shoulder and stalked out of the hotel.

Forget it. Just for tonight, she didn't want to be responsible. She didn't want to keep denying her needs. And she didn't want to always wonder how hot the sex might have been with Major Cole Jackson.

Too bad she'd turned him down.

COLE CRUISED around Vegas, his mind mulling over new strategies to make Jordan give in to him.

Never mind the challenge, he needed her. It had nothing to do with proving himself to his buddies. He just…needed her.

And it didn't take a brain surgeon to know she felt the same pull of desire he did. Their kiss had sparked every nerve ending he had, and he'd felt it igniting all through her and back into him.

But how to keep her from hitting the all-systems-off button again?

Winning was all about tactics. Tonight, he'd lost his cool and scared Jordan off. Bad habit. Leaping before he thought. Failing to curb his impulses. Same reason he'd gotten shot down.

As he pulled the Harley into the Grand's parking garage, he heard a screech of tires and a car horn honking. From the corner of his eye he caught a flash of red sequins in front of the honking cab. What the hell? Jordan was flipping the driver the bird as she strode past, heading back toward the hotel from the bus stop. And she was staring right at him.

Their gazes met. Her eyes flared. A tense energy radiated from her. My God. He was completely captivated. Her blond hair flowed around her shoulders, reminding him of a proud lioness.

He U-turned his bike into the exit lane and pulled up next to her.

There was a wild look in her eyes. "I'll take that ride now."

Suddenly, he couldn't think. Maybe it was all the blood rushing south. She wasn't usually in her work clothes at the bus stop. And she wasn't usually off this early. Something must have happened.

He shrugged out of his jacket, draped it over her shoulders and she slipped her arms in. Then he gestured for her to get on. "Where do you live?"

As she settled behind him, she wrapped her arms around his waist and her breasts pressed against his back. "I don't want to go home."

Her words socked him in the gut. "Where to, then?" He held his breath.

"Anywhere. Away from everything." Her voice trembled.

He could take her there and beyond. But he'd have to be a world-class jerk to take advantage of her in this mood. "Look, maybe you should—"

"Just get me out of here. Please." Her arms tightened and one hand roamed over his chest, the other down over his zipper.

His breathing hitched and his dick tried to jump into her palm. He clamped his jaw shut. "Zip the coat. The wind bites."

Her arms left him and he heard the zip, and when she

hugged him this time her hands spread across his stomach and chest. He checked the traffic, then roared out of the parking garage.

As Cole sped onto Las Vegas Boulevard, all he could think about was the heat, the slightest breath and movement, of her plastered against his back.

Once they passed the city limits she slid her hand under his belt and cupped his rock-hard cock through his briefs. And even though she hadn't moved her hand except to accommodate his lengthening, he was the most turned-on he'd ever been in his life. He felt as if one wrong move could have him begging for mercy.

Why hadn't he taken her straight up to his room? Because he'd heard the restlessness in her voice. She wanted to escape the hotel and everything it stood for. And so did he. Heading out into the desert night with her clinging tightly to him brought a primal urge to the surface—to haul his woman away from the world and keep her for himself.

With the eternal lights of Vegas only a glow on the horizon behind them, he slowed down, pulled off the road and into the dirt, and killed the engine. Beyond his headlight's beam, the sand and scrub disappeared into black nothingness, as if the rest of the world didn't exist. He could hear his ragged breathing, and hers. He could smell his desire. And hers.

He twisted to look at her, his hands squeezing the handlebars. Wondering if she'd leave him blue-balled, he searched her eyes.

She framed his face with her hands and pulled his

mouth to hers. Her kiss tasted of desperate hunger as she slipped her tongue inside.

Fumbling to kick down the bike stand, he took control of the kiss, taking it deep and wet. But she pulled away.

"This is just for tonight, right? Like you said—no promises."

"Uh…yeah, sure." At this point, he would have signed a contract in blood.

She nodded and slowly unzipped the jacket.

He unbuckled his belt, gripped her around the waist and pulled her in front of him, onto his lap. While she thrust her tongue deep into his mouth, she somehow straddled the seat to face him and hooked her legs over his thighs.

After that, things got frantic. Dug through his wallet for a condom. Ran his hands through her silky hair the way he'd been dreaming of. And never stopped kissing her. He couldn't get enough of her mouth and tongue, or her sweet, sexy whimpers.

Her hands were all over him, too. Her fingers combed through the hair at the back of his neck, and he shivered. She grabbed the edge of his T-shirt and lifted it to run her hands over his chest, tweaking his nipples until he wanted to squirm and beg. Then she roamed down to unbutton and unzip him and her fingers grazed his stiff, sensitive cock. Their mouths never breaking contact, she pulled down his briefs and encircled him. Sensations exploded. She stroked him with long, sensual pulls.

Oh, yes. His desire crested. He needed release. He needed to have her surrounding him.

Only vaguely aware that he'd moaned and growled like some crazed animal, he pushed into her caress. Then her hand and mouth were gone as she leaned back, yanked off his jacket and draped it over the handlebars. Closing her eyes, she pulled her top over her head, taking her bra with it. Thankful he'd left his headlight on, Cole licked his lips at the sight of her lush, round breasts. Blood pounded in his ears as he stared at her.

His cock twitching, he cupped her breasts and squeezed them, lifting one to his mouth. Her skin tasted sweet and salty and spicy all at once. Her nipples were perfect, large and dusky. He suckled and licked and buried his nose between the heavy mounds as he kissed their silken flesh.

He might never get enough of them. She was the ultimate high. One taste and he'd become a Jordan junkie.

As soon as the thought hit, his cock jumped and ached. He trailed kisses down to her quivering stomach, biting lightly, nibbling into her belly button and farther down to the edge of her panties. He wanted to be inside her now. "Take them off." With both hands, he gripped her waist and lifted her while she reached beneath her skirt and peeled them off, one long leg at a time. "Grip the bars behind you, and put your feet on my thighs." He cupped her butt and raised her warm pussy to his lips.

She was wet, so wet for him. He lapped at her sweet juice and licked her swollen clit, teasing it with gentle bites. He didn't know how much longer he'd last.

As he plunged his tongue in and played with her soft folds, she made little moaning sounds and called out.

He looked up to see her silhouetted against the light, her chest rising and falling, her hair blowing in the sandy breeze. Her eyes were squeezed closed, and the expression on her face as she opened them pierced him. He'd never had a woman come so fast.

He slid one hand up her damp back and she let go of the handlebars and wrapped her arms around his neck. Somehow he managed to slip the condom on before she slowly lowered herself onto his cock and he lost all reasonable thought.

She circled her legs around his hips and settled over him, wiggling into place.

"Don't move!" He gripped her hips, unsure how long he'd last in her tight warmth. His boot heels dug into the gravel. In this position he was buried to the hilt, yet he couldn't push up into her, couldn't pump into her the way his body screamed for him to.

With a mischievous smile, she pressed her lips to his neck and trailed kisses up behind his ear, down his jaw and finally covered his mouth.

She made him frantic, mad for release. He lost control. He gripped her butt and raised and lowered her. Soon she caught the rhythm and braced her arms on his shoulders to rock her hips.

Indescribable pleasure washed over him, building stronger, faster, hitting him harder. He held on tight, and a strangled cry escaped as he shot deep into her core. Hits of ecstasy bombarded his groin and spread up his entire body.

Her fingers clenched on his scalp and scraped down

his back as he tried to regain his breath. Echoes of the thrill still tingled and stung. He looked up and found Venus on the western horizon and Mars hanging just above the crescent moon. He picked out the Pleiades, Canis Captain and Orion. Anything to take his mind off the fact that he was squeezing Jordan to him as if his life depended on her and his eyes had come damn close to watering until he'd blinked a couple times.

Anything to forget that he didn't want to let go.

4

THREE HOURS later Cole pulled his Harley into a parking space next to McCabe's Jeep at Red Rocks National Conservation Area. The sun was inching its way over the canyons to the east, and Cole sat staring at the orange and purple streaks coloring the clouds.

He wished he was up there, above the stratosphere. He wished he'd never come to Vegas. After the hospital, he should have gone straight to Phoenix to visit his folks.

Why the hell did he feel as if he'd lost the bet instead of won it? He was supposed to relish the look on McCabe's face when Cole told him he'd gotten lucky with the Keno girl.

But she wasn't just a Keno girl. She was a woman. A woman who'd been upset enough to ride off with him on his bike and do something she'd told him only a few hours earlier that she couldn't do. And he hadn't even found out why. He'd just taken what she offered.

McCabe climbed out of his Jeep, sipping steaming coffee from a cup. "Why aren't you dressed? You can't wear— Wait a minute. Isn't that the same shirt you had on last night?"

Cole glanced at his shirt. "So it is." Swinging a leg off the bike, he ignored McCabe's searching gaze, reached into the back of the Jeep and pulled out harnesses and ropes.

"You been out all night? Tell me you didn't…"

Cole suppressed a smug grin. "All right. I didn't." He grabbed the backpack full of their climbing shoes and gloves from the Jeep and nodded to Grady, who'd just pulled up in his truck.

"Well, I'll be. Grady, he did it! He nailed Ms. Crash-and-Burn."

"Don't call her that."

McCabe grinned. "Guess we can't anymore. From now on, we'll have to call her Ms. For-a-Good-Ti—"

Cole jerked him up by his T-shirt. "Shut up."

McCabe stared at him with a puzzled expression. "Okay, Jackson. One good screw and she's got you pussy-whipped? Didn't you learn anything from my mistake?"

"Just because you married a whore—"

McCabe broke Cole's hold and slammed a fist into his jaw.

Cole stumbled back against his bike and pushed off again, fist swinging.

Grady stepped between them, caught Cole's knuckles in his palm, and shoved the two buddies apart. "You want to fight, take it somewhere else." He looked pointedly at the family scrambling out of a minivan with backpacks and hiking boots. "I'll be on the western cliff." He picked up his harness and rope and strode away.

Cole let his breathing slow, rubbing a hand over his stinging jaw.

"I got an extra pair of shorts in the Jeep," McCabe mumbled.

Cole nodded. "Thanks."

Turning to pull another backpack from the vehicle, McCabe shook his head. "What can I say? I'm an ass." He grinned. "I was just pissed you made it with a woman who turned me down flat."

A slow grin spread across Cole's face as he unbuttoned his dress shirt. "No. You're pissed because now you have to be a monk for the next thirty days."

McCabe groaned and cursed under his breath.

"I NEED A sit-rep, Jackson," Grady called down to Cole.

Cole used his T-shirt-covered shoulder to soak up the sweat dripping off his forehead. He was clinging to a measly grade-two slope, shaking so hard he could barely hold on to the rock face. If it weren't for the harness, he'd have already fallen the thirty feet he'd managed to climb. And Grady wanted a situation report? Hell, couldn't he see for himself?

"Hey, Jackson." McCabe lowered himself back down to Cole's side. "It's no big deal. Let's head down for a beer."

"No. I'm fine." This wasn't over. Cole set his jaw and raised his foot to the next crevice.

Ignore the vertigo, Jackson. Push past the dizziness and nausea.

How many times had he and his buddies climbed

these canyons? And he'd always been the first one to the top. Once there, he'd lie on his back and stare at the vivid blue sky, feel the sun dry his drenched shirt, and give the rest of the guys hell for being so slow.

And now look at him.

It was the ear injury that screwed up his equilibrium. Same reason the flight surgeon had permanently revoked his flying privileges.

"Jackson, you got nothing to prove here, buddy."

"I'm not quitting." He glanced up to find his next handhold and the world started spinning again as if he was in a centrifuge chair. The next thing to come into focus was McCabe's face. He had an arm around Cole's back, keeping him upright and he looked…concerned.

Goddammit.

"You can stay on the side of this mountain if you want." McCabe let go of him, began releasing the tension in his rope. "But I only have four more days of leave." He rappeled down a couple of feet. "I don't know why I let you talk me into this much work. Time for some fun." He looked at Cole. "How about we watch Grady pay off his part of the bet? I can't wait to see him in a mud mask and cucumber slices." He grinned.

As distractions went, the image had a certain appeal. But Cole burned with frustration. McCabe was only trying to save his pride.

Too late for that.

Something inside him shriveled as he made the decision to loosen his rope and follow McCabe down the mountain.

What was he supposed to do with the rest of his life? He probably couldn't shoot the Colorado rapids, either. Or hang glide over the Hoover. What was left for him? Some vanilla desk-jockey job? He'd go insane.

And he'd never forget the expression on his dad's face at the hospital when he'd heard the news. Though he'd tried to take his son's grounding in stride, General James Jackson, retired Air Force, had seemed…shaken.

Maybe Cole should have just stayed in that Iraqi desert and let the buzzards take him. At least then he might have died a hero, instead of ending up some paunchy, pasty, paper-pusher.

That was crazy thinking. Self-pity was for cowards. And so was giving up. He'd almost reached the ground and jumped the last few feet, landing with a thud that sounded a death knell to his climbing days. He shook off the thought and started gathering up his rope, winding it into a neat loop around his hand and elbow. He'd served his country. He'd thrived on the challenges of combat. And he'd known the risks. He should be thankful. He was damned lucky to be alive.

And life was for living to the fullest. There were other challenges for him. He still had his bike and he still had—

The memory of Jordan naked in the dark desert washed over him like a cool cleansing waterfall. The feel of her gorgeous breasts pushed against his chest, and his hands clasping her butt as she rode him as if he was a bronc at the championship rodeo. He shivered, although the temperature must have been ninety-plus degrees.

Women. That was one adventure still left to him.

Wouldn't it kill McCabe to see Cole take a beautiful woman to his room, knowing he couldn't have one for another month?

He went and stood next to McCabe. "Hell, maybe I'll open that whiskey after all."

MONDAY AFTERNOON Jordan dragged herself into work at The Grand thankful that she was off tomorrow. As she entered the females' dressing room she caught Sherri bent over, adjusting her cleavage for maximum effect.

Jordan told her, "I'm never taking your advice again."

Sherri glanced up at Jordan's words, and then did a double take. "Oh. My. Gawd. You got laid!"

Jordan's face flamed as she dropped her backpack on a bench. "And yet." She glared at her misguided friend. "I still might not pass differential equations."

"Oh, hon, what happened?" Sherri grabbed her arms for a quick hug. "Was it that gorgeous scarred major?"

Jordan blinked. "Focus, Sherri. My finals? You said sex would relax me so I could study. But now I can't concentrate at all. And I can't sleep."

"Yeah, yeah. Like you really have to worry, Ms. Brainiac." Sherri sat on the bench and crossed her arms and legs. "Now tell me all about Mr. Tall-Dark-and-Mm-mm-mm. He was asking about you, you know."

"What? When?"

Sherri raised her brows and gave a smug smile. "Saturday. Wanted to know all about how long you'd worked here and what you did for fun. And Kayla told me that last night she saw the guy with his tongue down your throat right outside these doors. And then you left early…"

Good grief, Sherri should start her own detective agency. "I—I don't know what I was thinking. I just lost it." Jordan sat down and pulled off her sneakers.

Sherri squealed and clasped her hands to her chest. "Tell. Tell!"

Jordan shook her head. No way would she share the experience. It was beyond description. She'd never been so sexually aggressive. And on a motorcycle? A sweet, aching throb hit her core as she remembered.

The wild ride with the engine vibrating between her legs, and the major's hardening erection in her palm. The feel of his large hands cupping her breasts, his lips tugging at her nipples. And—oh—his mouth on her clit. She didn't want to think about how he'd gained the experience to be so good. She'd just appreciate being the recipient of such talent. Even if the after-sex part had been rather awkward.

"Sweet heavenly choir, Jordan! You should see your face. Must have been one hell of a night," Sherri exclaimed.

With a cleansing intake of breath, Jordan returned to the present. "Let's call it temporary insanity and leave it at that." She glanced at the time clock and started changing into her uniform.

"You're not going to see him again? Why not?"

"Sherri, you're the one who said I didn't have to have a commitment to 'get me some.' "

"Commitment schmitment." Sherri pursed her lips

and waved a hand. "I'm guessing he's only got a week's leave." She shrugged. "So, you have one more for the road, where's the harm?" She stood and moved to the mirror to touch up her lipstick. "You got the next two days off, don't you?"

As Jordan finished getting into her uniform, she tried to pinpoint the reason for her second thoughts after she'd gotten home last night. Where was the harm? Didn't sex so amazing warrant a second go around?

No, no. She had finals to study for. And even if she didn't, once, she could chalk up to an impulsive, hormonal indulgence. Blowing off some steam. But, seeing him again? She'd never forget his final shudder in her arms as they both slowly recovered from their shattering orgasms. Her hand in his hair, his nose touching her neck. She'd felt so close to him. As if he'd shown her a side of himself no one else saw. But that was ridiculous. Except….

Neither of them had spoken as he disposed of the condom and adjusted his jeans. Nor as he'd helped her find her uniform top and bra while she stepped into her panties. Except for giving him directions to her apartment, nothing else had been said between them.

No, "See ya later." No, "I'll call you." No goodbye kiss.

Just an odd expression crossing his face as she handed him his jacket after she got off his bike in the apartment complex. The look in his dark eyes had been almost…regretful. But that didn't make sense. He'd gotten what he wanted, hadn't he? He'd said no strings. And she wasn't complaining. Those rules suited her fine. She hadn't been angling for anything more. Just a good, honest, mutually satisfying night of incredible sex.

Then why, as she headed for the casino, did she feel so unsatisfied?

"HOW ABOUT the babe at eleven o'clock?" McCabe asked, nodding toward a lustrous brunette at the roulette wheel.

Cole gestured for the Blackjack dealer to hit him one more time and then checked her out. Nice curves. Sultry eyes. Winked at him.

"Nah. Too easy."

"What the— Ah you kiddin'?" McCabe's Southern drawl deepened in direct proportion to how much booze he'd tossed back. He gestured to the dealer for another card and busted. Grumbling a slurred curse, he finished his tumbler of vodka and threw in his cards. "Too short. Too tall. Too thin. Too fat. Now, too easy? You're killing me, man."

"What's it to you, Mon Man?" Cole shot back. He lifted the corners of his cards again. Even twenty. He held his palm up, signaling the dealer he had enough.

"First the voodoo lady's shop is closed on Mondays, so Grady can't get his massage, and now you've suddenly turned into Mistah Picky." McCabe quipped and turned to order another drink from a passing waitress.

Hughes appeared and intercepted the waitress, who nodded and walked off.

"Hey," McCabe complained. "I wanted anothah drink."

"You've had enough. I ordered you coffee." Hughes crossed her arms over her chest.

"You did what? Aw, come on. I thought you were my friend."

Cole gestured to the empty stool next to him, but Hughes shook her head, maintaining her defensive stance between them.

Her eyes narrowed and her lip curled. "You're your own worst enemy, Mitch."

"The hell I am." McCabe spun on his stool and poked a finger in Hughes's chest. "I just lost a bet because of you."

"What are you talking about? You mean that Keno girl actually slept with Jackson?"

"Don't act so innocent," cajoled McCabe. "The only way Ms. Crash-and-Burn would have slept with Cole after only knowing him three days—" McCabe slowly stood "—is if you told her about the bet and then y'all cooked up a scheme for her to do him. Jus' because I fluhted with her a little, she had to get revenge? Well, what'd I evah do to you, huh?" By the end of his tirade he was swaying and several people were staring. Hughes looked about ready to break a glass over his head.

"I had nothing to do with you losing a bet, you jackass," she ground out between her teeth. "But I almost wish I had."

"I thought you were different, Hughes." McCabe's tone changed. "I thought you were one of us."

"Yeah, well, that's your mistake, McCabe." Hughes poked him in the chest. "Thinking I'm not a woman."

McCabe pushed her finger away. "You're not," he mumbled.

Hughes's eyes narrowed into furious slits. "What did you say?"

McCabe tipped sideways. Though he was twice her size, Hughes caught him. Deep concern crossed her features before she flattened her expression again.

What had that look been about? If Cole didn't know better… He stood and placed his hand on McCabe's back. "Hey, buddy. Let's see if we can catch a game on TV in the bar."

McCabe swung around to him, his eyes wide and unfocused. "I thought she was one of us, Jackson."

"I'll take him home," Hughes volunteered. She glanced at Cole, her arms still holding McCabe up. "Grab his keys, would you? He can't drive like this."

"I can take him." Cole reached into McCabe's jacket pocket.

Hughes shook her head. "You stay. I'm ready to get out of here. He can catch a ride back into town tomorrow and retrieve his car." She looked up at McCabe. "Mitch, I'm taking you home, buddy."

"Okay." He threw his arm over her shoulders, his accusations evidently forgotten. "Won't be the first time, eh, Hughes?" He shot her an evil grin.

Cole handed Hughes McCabe's keys. "I'll see you tomorrow."

Hughes nodded and headed for the exit with McCabe leaning heavily on her.

Cole glanced at his watch. About time for shift change.

He scooped up his pack of chips and stood, scanning the room for—yeah, okay, so he was looking for her.

Who said it had to be a different woman every night? That was McCabe's rule, right? Just because he'd been hurt by his ex. So what if Cole wanted to hook up with the same woman more than once? The conditions would still apply. No strings. Just a good time.

A hell of a good time.

He just hadn't gotten enough of her yet, that's all. It'd happened so fast. This time they'd go up to his room, have space to move around. Take it slow and easy on a soft bed, and maybe he'd order some wine and a midnight dinner and they'd slip into the bathtub after, and then they'd do it all over again.

He was hard just thinking about the things he wanted to do to her.

Carrying his chips under his arm, he made his way around the perimeter of the casino looking for Jordan, and the more ground he covered without seeing her, the more his stomach knotted.

A siren of ringing bells and flashing lights signaled someone had hit the jackpot at the slots. The noise irritated him, drowned out any other sound, and he recognized he'd have to get used to loud noises making him virtually deaf.

Like a starving desert coyote on the hunt for elusive prey, he checked the Keno betting booths, wandered to the chips counter and cashed in, and then strolled over to the employees' entrance. Every time he spotted a waitress in a red uniform he'd do a double take, but it was never Jordan. Annoyance scratched along his nerves as he paced back to the roulette wheel. Still no sign of her.

A fever burned inside him. Where was she? The longer he stalked her, the more his heart pounded, the more his blood rushed through his veins and a sweat broke out on his upper lip. To hell with this. She had to be here. He felt like a desperate man, betting everything he owns on one last role of the dice, as he grabbed a chair, stepped up onto it and scanned the room.

"UM...JORDAN." Sherri tapped her shoulder. "Look."

Something in Sherri's tone set the fine hairs on the back of Jordan's neck tingling. Sherri sounded half excited, half frightened. Jordan gave the lady from Texas her Keno cards and change, accepting a generous tip, and then slowly turned.

Her breathing hitched, and then failed altogether. The noise of the casino retreated, her surroundings faded. She swallowed as she stared across the room. Cole.

His intense gaze might as well have been armor-piercing. His dark eyes sent an unspoken message: I want you. And now she knew the power in that body, barely restrained, that lay beneath his leather jacket. The passion waiting to be unleashed in those strong arms. The expertise of his mouth. As she stood there he disappeared from sight, and she knew he was coming for her.

Her mind screamed, *Run. Escape.* Now, while she could. But her legs wouldn't move. Her feet had become lead weights anchored to the carpet. She looked to Sherri for support, but her supposed friend had deserted her, strolling off into the crowd to sell Keno cards. Traitor.

When Jordan turned back Cole was standing before

her. She gasped a giant breath of air into her deprived lungs and her senses filled with the height and width of him. The musk of his aftershave, the starch of his shirt, the roughness of his jaw. And his eyes a pure, rich brown.

"I still want you," he rasped, then winced, as if he couldn't believe what he'd just admitted.

"I—I'm working." She was hot, restless.

"After your shift."

She glanced down, saw his fists clench and unclench. Saw the ridge behind his zipper. She closed her eyes to block the intense feelings.

One more for the road. Should she? Could she handle the aftermath?

He reached up and fingered a curly lock of hair just below her shoulder. "I'm in Tower One. Sixteen-oh-two." His knuckles grazed the skin above her breast.

She shivered.

"Will you come up?" He twined the curl around his index finger and stared at the ringlet as if it was water and he'd been dying of thirst.

Yes was on the tip of her tongue. She knew how good it would be between them, rolling around on a bed, skin to skin everywhere this time. His touch would scorch. His kiss would incinerate. She sensed there were currents of emotion he kept under tight control. He might leave her burned, but he'd never leave her cold and indifferent.

Yet she couldn't afford to be burned again. Wanting someone this badly couldn't be good. This kind of craving led to obsession, to disastrous decisions.

Come on, Jordan. Use your intellect. What were the

odds that this guy had the potential to completely devastate what was left of her common sense? Too high. She was smarter than that, wasn't she?

He ran the back of his fingers softly across her collarbone, moving lower.

Her skin prickled with awareness. One more night.

"Your skin is so soft." He looked up, his brows drawn tightly together. "And you smell so good."

She closed her eyes, knowing she was about to give in. She still wanted him, too.

"Hughes told ya 'bout the bet, din' she?" Captain McCabe stumbled against Jordan.

She blinked and looked at him. "Bet?"

"McCabe." Cole inserted himself between them. "Shut. Up." He ground the words between his teeth.

The captain tapped his temple with his index finger and winked. "She convinced ya ta sleep with Jackson so I'd lose, right?"

A sharp pain stabbed Jordan in the chest. "What?" Her eyes stung. Cole had only seduced her to win a bet…

"Mitch." A petite female soldier in shapeless camos stalked up and gripped the captain's shoulder. "Come on, Mitch. You're wasted, buddy."

"I just want the truth!" Captain McCabe said loudly.

Heads turned. Jordan backed away. Humiliation blazed in her face and gut.

"Jordan." Cole grabbed her arm. "Let me explain."

She jerked out of his grasp.

He reached for her again but the woman soldier, a captain also by her insignia, grabbed his wrist. "Let her be, Jackson. Why don't you take McCabe home? He won't listen to me."

Thankful for the woman's interference, Jordan drew in a deep breath and glanced at her floor supervisor, who was edging closer toward Captain McCabe. She couldn't afford for her boss to witness another scene. Even worse, she couldn't face Cole. Couldn't think. She should have trusted her instincts, known there was more to his intense seduction.

"You really didn't know about the bet?" Captain McCabe murmured as he swayed to one side and Cole caught him.

"Not until just now, you ass," the female captain snapped at him.

Her nails digging into her palms, Jordan avoided looking at Cole as she took another step back. "I have to work." She turned and made a hasty escape into the protective shroud of the casino.

Footsteps sounded behind her, solid footsteps, but lighter than the major's heavy trod. Jordan turned to see the woman captain following. "I'm really sorry about all that."

"No problem." Jordan only wanted to forget the whole thing. Weaving in between slot machines, she increased her stride, making her way to the Keno lounge.

But the woman kept pace with her. "Major Jackson's a good man, Ms. Brenner."

Without pausing, Jordan glanced at the female captain. "Right. 'Cause only good men have sex with a woman on a bet."

"Not worthy of an airman, I agree. But his recent injuries have changed him."

Jordan stopped. "What do you mean? How?"

The woman stuck out her right hand. "I'm Captain Hughes," she said, then shrugged. "Alexandria."

Feeling as if she'd stepped into a bizarre reality show, Jordan shook her hand. "Jordan. So, how have Cole's injuries changed him?"

Captain Hughes—Alexandria—narrowed one eye and drew in a deep breath, then clasped her hands behind her back. "I think that's something Jackson would need to tell you himself."

5

AS SHE SAT IN HER OFFICE on base the next morning, Captain Alexandria Hughes practically rubbed her hands together in glee. Mitch McCabe, the ladies' man of Las Vegas, had finally, incredibly, got what was coming to him. A month of forced celibacy.

And just to make sure Mitch's thirty days without a woman wasn't wasted, Alex was going to take advantage of his predicament and use it for a little payback.

Last month McCabe had sent a strip-o-gram to her office on her thirtieth birthday. That was only the most recent in a series of devious plots and outrageous pranks that had been going on for twelve years.

They'd been springing practical jokes on each other since they were cadets at the academy. One of the worst was when McCabe got her arrested in Guam for solicitation of a male prostitute. She'd sweated it out in that holding cell for more than three hours before McCabe showed up with a shit-eating grin and let her know the MPs were in on the prank.

But she'd had her revenge. One night a few months later she'd spiked his beer and he'd woken up handcuffed to his bed, wearing women's lingerie. His hair had been dyed hot pink and his nails—fingers and toes—painted to match. McCabe had refused to drink anything she handed him for years after that.

Now, Mitch's cell phone—with all those women's numbers he kept in there—called to her from her desk drawer, begging her to use it. In the struggle to help him to her car last night she'd snatched it from his pocket and he hadn't even noticed.

Oh, she knew about the stored phone numbers. Even before his marriage he'd been a ladies' man, handsome and charming. And women would leave their numbers on whatever available surface they could find. But, he'd been different back then. He'd always been mischievous, but he'd never been malicious. It wasn't until after his divorce that he'd turned into this new, callous Mitch. The player, the serial dater trying to screw everything in a skirt to get even for the way he'd been screwed.

Only Alex knew everything Luanne had done to him. What the ugly divorce had cost Mitch.

But enough was enough. It was time for him to get over it. And him losing this bet afforded her the perfect opportunity to give Captain Mitchell Lee McCabe a taste of his own medicine.

Alex grabbed his cell phone out of her drawer, snapped it open, and began working her way through his phone book.

MORE NERVOUS than he cared to admit, Cole strode up the walkway to Jordan's apartment.

He had to apologize. And, yeah, maybe he just didn't like to admit defeat, but he hadn't given up on the whole dinner-and-bath-in-his-hotel-room idea. Luckily, she was off today. Maybe seeing him away from the casino would help.

He raised a fist and knocked on her door.

It opened too fast for her to have checked the peephole and he made a mental note to caution her about opening the door without looking to see who it was first. This rundown apartment complex wasn't in the best neighborhood.

The shocked expression on her face wasn't exactly encouraging.

"What are you doing here?"

"I'm sorry. The bet was…juvenile."

She glanced nervously into the apartment, then stepped outside and closed the door, gripping the doorknob.

Did she have a guy in there? Had she brought someone home with her last night? It was a crazy thought, but it made his hands itch to reach around her and shove open the door.

She looked up at him, squinting into the noon sun, and he studied her more closely. Her face was free of makeup and there were dark circles under her eyes. Her hair was pulled back in a ponytail and she wore an over-size T-shirt and cut-off shorts.

"Captain McCabe was right. I knew all about your bet and—" she faltered exactly the way she had the night she'd tried to convince him she had five kids, and then she recovered, raising her chin defiantly "—decided to teach him a lesson. Anyway—" she drew in a deep breath "—you can leave with a clear conscience." She stepped back inside and tried to shut the door.

He planted a hand on the door above her head and leaned close. "Jordan. Believe me. My wanting you had nothing to do with a bet." Staring into her violet eyes, he shook his head. "I still want you."

Just before her expression hardened, he thought he caught a flash of pain in her eyes.

"Help!"

Jordan flinched at the female screech from inside the apartment. "You need to leave," Jordan insisted, shoving the door closed in his face.

"Help me!" The screamer sounded terrified. Whatever was going on, he wasn't leaving until he knew Jordan was safe. He pushed the door open, prepared to fight.

Jordan swung around and gaped at him, but the stunned look morphed into a furious glare. She had her arm around a crying older woman. "It's okay, Mom. I'm here."

Jordan's mother?

She was beautiful. An older version of Jordan. Her hair was disheveled and she clutched a ratty robe to her throat. She looked scared. Fragile. "Who are you?" she asked Jordan. "Why are you keeping me here?" She pulled away from her daughter and her bottom lip trembled.

"I'm Jordie, Mom. Remember? You live here. I was just— Someone was at the door."

For the first time, the woman looked up at Cole, fear in her eyes.

Cole smiled and extended his right hand. "I'm Cole, a friend of your daughter's. Nice to meet you, ma'am."

The woman shrank from his hand and whimpered.

Jordan shot him an irritated scowl. "Cole was just leaving." She raised her brows and glanced pointedly at the door.

Instead of leaving, Cole scanned the tiny apartment. It was spotlessly clean, but contained only a minimum of furniture. The living-room furnishings consisted of an old sofa with a neatly folded blanket and pillow at one end, and a small TV with a scarred coffee table as a stand. Under the front window sat a little dining table and two chairs marking the entrance to a miniscule galley kitchen. Textbooks and notebooks lay scattered on the table. Jordan's university books.

Beyond the front room a short hallway led to two doors. He guessed a bedroom and a bathroom. Did Jordan sleep on the couch? "Actually," he improvised, "I came to ask you two beautiful women to lunch." He smiled at Jordan's mother. "Ma'am?"

"Oh." The woman smiled.

"No." Jordan spoke firmly. "We're not dressed. Besides. I don't think we'd all fit on your bike."

Damn. He hadn't thought of that.

"But I can get dressed." Her mother began finger-combing her hair. "I'd like to go out. It's been a long time since a man asked me out." Her voice trailed off and her face took on a faraway expression.

Jordan left her side and began pushing Cole toward the door. "My mom doesn't do well in public," she said quietly. "And I have to study for finals this week. Now, please. Go."

Cole glanced back at Jordan's beautiful, ill mother and something inside him shifted. His throat constricted and he let himself be shoved over the threshold. "I'm sorry. I didn't know."

Jordan's eyes sparked with anger. "I don't need your pity. I just need you to leave me alone." Then she slammed the door in his face.

UNBELIEVABLE. Some guys just didn't know when to quit.

He thought he could just come over here and stare at her with those deep-brown eyes, smelling all manly, and tell her he still wanted her and expect her to fall into his arms?

Jordan spent a half hour soothing her mother's tantrum and finally got her settled on the sofa watching *All My Children*.

This wasn't the first time her mom had forgotten her. But every time Mom looked at her as if she was a stranger, Jordan felt as if she'd lost a piece of who she was. Her usual pragmatism had seen her through a lot the past few years. But it ripped out a chunk of her soul to think about the future.

She stared at a can of chicken soup in one hand and a can of tuna in the other. But she had no appetite, and her mother had refused to eat.

Replacing both cans in the cabinet, she dropped into

a kitchen chair, opened her notebook, and tried to concentrate. But the words blurred, and she closed her stinging eyes.

She'd lain awake a long time last night trying to persuade herself there was no reason to feel humiliated. After all, it had been her choice to go with him on his bike. Her decision to have sex. And she'd gone into it knowing it would be a one-night stand. So what if he'd only pursued her because of a bet? For a few hours she'd been carefree and irresponsible. And the sex had sizzled.

But deep down was a pinprick of pain she couldn't reason away. She'd been seduced—literally—by the fantasy. Again. Somehow, her twisted psyche had believed Cole had wanted the real Jordan. Not just the leggy blonde with C cups, but the person on the inside. Her pencil snapped in her hands. All those sincere lines about wanting to get to know her. Hah! She'd been suckered into feeling a connection with the guy. And she only had herself to blame.

She jumped when the doorbell rang. What now? She'd never get any studying done at this rate.

As she swung open the door, her breath caught.

Cole gripped three bulging plastic grocery bags in each hand. His mouth was set in a determined line. "If I can't take you to lunch, I'll bring lunch to you." He pushed past her without an invitation.

"Cole." She followed him into the kitchen where he began unpacking the bags. Deli meats and cheeses, whole wheat bread, lettuce, tomatoes, fresh fruit… Her stomach rumbled so loudly even the TV couldn't drown out the sound. "I really can't accept— Is that pasta salad?"

He grinned as he glanced at the clear plastic container. "You like?" He bent to search through her cabinets and drawers, pulling out plates and silverware, and a chopping board. "Do you have a—ah, perfect!" He held up a large kitchen knife.

Her pulse sped up at his warm smile.

Ooh, that was exactly how she'd weakened the last time. She had to stay strong. Unmoved.

But his eyes twinkled with mischief as he looked at her, and a lock of dark brown hair fell over his forehead as he shrugged out of his jacket. Beneath was another perfectly starched button-down shirt, a deep blue this time. It was tucked neatly into low-riding jeans that hugged his butt and long legs.

But she wasn't falling for that devilish smile and perfect butt. She wasn't.

"You don't have to do this. I don't need your charity—"

"Jordan." Her name sounded so sexy as it rumbled in his deep voice. He shifted his weight and folded his arms. And he looked at her. His gaze didn't drift once to her breasts, but stared solemnly into her eyes, as if he really saw her. "They're only sandwiches."

Yeah, he'd said the same thing about the ice cream and look where that had gotten her.

She was too aware of his large frame moving around, overwhelming the space, overwhelming her senses. She continued to stand there as he unbuttoned his sleeves, rolled them up and washed his hands at the sink. She remembered the feel of them on her breasts and caressing her back, clutching her hips… She swallowed.

Oh, she was doing it again. She should throw him out. He was only trying to relieve his own guilt. And she didn't want some pity-lunch.

Her mother breezed into the kitchen, grinning as if Cole was a regular visitor in their home. While he sliced the tomato, she poured him a glass of iced tea and— there was no other word for it—she flirted. Like a young girl with a teenage crush.

Jordan watched in utter fascination. She'd never known her dad. He'd left before she was even born. But she suddenly saw her mom as she must have been before she'd been burdened with an unwanted pregnancy and a paycheck-to-paycheck life as a single mother.

Tammy Lynn Brenner was lovely. Moving in sync with Cole as they put sandwiches together, she dimpled and looked up at him from beneath her lashes. Not overtly sexual, but simply…sensual, yet without guile.

Jordan found herself sitting at the kitchen table while Mom served her tea and a sandwich as if she were waiting on customers back at the diner in Iowa. Maybe she shouldn't have moved her mom out here when she got sick. Maybe Jordan should have tried to find a job in Cedar Falls.

Cole set the bowls of fruit and pasta salad in the center of the table, wiping his hands on a dish towel. "Let's eat." He pulled the other chair out for her mother, and then hopped up on the counter with his plate.

Jordan bit into her sandwich and closed her eyes as her mouth watered. She'd been starving.

"So, you have finals this week?" Cole asked.

"Yes. Tomorrow and Thursday." And, she hoped, by Friday she'd know how she'd done.

"What's your major?"

"Computer Science. I hope to find something in programming or IT support."

As he asked her more, she told him about how she'd researched the market before deciding on a career field and how a few years ago the number of IT companies in Vegas had increased. But now, she might have to look in other cities. The subject changed to the once booming housing market in the suburbs, and how it seemed to have dropped off in the past couple of years, forcing many military families out of rentals that were being foreclosed.

Every few moments she'd sneak a peek at Cole. Watching him eat was torturous. His mouth closing around the sandwich, his jaw muscles tightening as he chewed. She shouldn't be this captivated. But his firm thighs covered by tight jeans were right in front of her and she found it impossible to stop her gaze from straying to the significant bulge between them.

He cleared his throat and she glanced up into his eyes. He knew she'd been staring at his crotch. Her cheeks burned. *Oh, please let the earth swallow me up now.*

"Did you want to play, too?" her mom asked.

Jordan blinked. "I'm sorry. What were we talking about?"

"Tammy and I are going to play some Gin," Cole answered.

"Oh." Jordan checked the time. "I'm sure Cole has other things to do." If she weren't such an idiot she'd have gone back to the bedroom and studied instead of wasting time drooling over some smooth operator. "But you and I can play, Mom." With a longing glance at her class notes, she stood and stacked the plates. "As soon as I do these dishes, okay?"

Cole jumped off the counter as she rose. "I've got these." He took the plates from her and grabbed the silverware with his other hand. "Why don't you go study?" The unwavering look in his eyes softened as he flashed that devilish smile at her mother and took two strides to the sink. "I'll wash if you dry, Tammy."

Her mother simpered as she got to her feet, picking up napkins and tea glasses. She turned a wondrous look to Jordan. "He's such a hunk," she whispered like a schoolgirl as she followed him.

Jordan's face flamed. She couldn't let him bring lunch and wash the dishes. She opened her mouth and then closed it. Her mother had thrown a fit earlier when Jordan had made him leave. Resentment flared. Why did she have to be the bad guy and Cole got to be Mr. Charming Hunk making nice with her mom? Playing the role of hero, stepping in to save the day. She didn't need rescuing. They were just fine without him.

She watched her mom smiling and laughing with Cole. Having fun for the first time in a long time.

And the truth was, she did need some quiet time to

study. Would it hurt to accept help just this once? It wasn't as if she was depending on him for any kind of long-term commitment.

Spine stiffening, she gathered up her notebooks and textbooks. Cole looked up from washing a plate and stared at her. She met his dark gaze and the back of her neck tingled. The room felt hot, suffocating. She knew—she just knew—he was remembering that night on his motorcycle. His hands on her body, his mouth buried between her thighs. Him, inside her.

At the memory, her cotton panties were wet. Before he could read the need on her face, she ducked her head and strode into the bedroom.

6

"YOU GOT a personal problem, Jackson?" Lieutenant Colonel Ethan Grady barked the question like the drill sergeant he used to be as he straddled the stool next to Cole's. Even if Grady hadn't approached him on his good side, Cole would have heard him.

Cole swigged the last of his Cuervo and let the final strains of George Jones's "I'll Always Get Lucky With You" end before he acknowledged him. "Besides you?"

"You were supposed to meet us at that yoga lady's shop after lunch." Grady waved the bartender over. "Soda water. No ice."

"Oh." Cole signaled for another shot of Cuervo.

"'Oh'? That's it? You risked your uncle's fifty-year-old Scotch to make me get a herbal treatment and then you don't even show?"

"So, did the lady help you find your chi?" Cole sucked down the next shot of Cuervo.

Grady took a sip of his water. "Nope. We'll have to reschedule. Figured you needed to be there since you won the bet." He set down his drink and turned to face Cole. "Where you been the last twelve hours?"

Where had he been? Some alternate universe, maybe? That was the only explanation for why he'd knocked on Jordan's door intent on seduction and then settled for domestic duties. He'd played Gin all afternoon with a poor lady who was losing her mind. And left without making a move on Jordan. Not even a kiss on the cheek as she'd shown him to the door. Maybe he was losing his mind, too.

Grady's hand clamped on his shoulder. "You okay?"

Cole noted Grady's worried gaze. He was sick of people looking at him like that. "I'm good."

Trying to clear his mind, he'd ridden out to Hoover Dam after leaving Jordan's and watched some guys kayaking down Black Canyon. He'd shot those rapids before. But never again. The knowledge burned a hole only tequila could fill. Or Jordan.

No. He had to shake the whole Jordan thing off. She was just a Keno girl he'd had a good time with. There'd been plenty before her. And there'd be plenty after. So she'd treated him as if they were nothing more than polite strangers when he'd left this afternoon. He'd never wanted to get involved with the woman anyway. Relationships tied a man down. Just ask his dad.

What he needed was to get his head straight. Get back in the saddle, as his grandfather would have said. He'd apologized to Jordan, right?

He gulped his Cuervo, slammed the tumbler on the bar, and stood. "I only got a few days left. Let's go find some women."

Grady's brows shot up, but he finished his water and then followed Cole upstairs to Studio 54.

Even on a Tuesday night at one in the morning, The Grand's largest nightclub buzzed with energy. The throbbing bass vibrated in Cole's chest, half-naked go-go girls danced in cages, strobe lights flickered on the dance floor crowded with women. The thunderous music rendered him deaf to human voices, but then probably everyone in here was.

Forgetting Grady, he shouldered his way to the dance floor where half a dozen women were gyrating to the pounding rhythm. Their arms raised, they bumped against each other, but smiled as he joined them.

He smiled back.

One of them moved in front of him and slid her palm down his shirt front. Another came from behind and grabbed his butt. Oh, yeah. This is what he needed. He leaned down to ask the one in front her name and she stabbed her nails into his hair and bit his earlobe.

He jerked away.

A woman behind him grabbed his arm and he turned to find a curvy redhead. He slid his hand down her spine to the top of her sweet round bottom, intent on kissing her. But her makeup seemed packed on and her perfume was too sharp, too spicy.

He turned to a dark-skinned beauty. Ahh, yes. A fiery *señorita* was just what he needed. She smiled at him, but he closed his eyes and let his other senses take over. The heat of her soft body crushed against him. The feel of her hands slipping under his jacket and running over his shoulders. He tried to conjure images of the *señorita* in his bed. But all he could picture were long blond curls spread over his pillow.

What was wrong with him?

He spun on his heel and pushed past the dancing women, his throat tight. His temples pounding in frustration, he headed for the exit.

Grady stood close to the door, his arms folded, and his face expressionless. Suddenly, Grady's unfailing composure infuriated Cole. The man never drank. Never swore. Never lost control, while Cole's life had been in a crazy tailspin ever since he'd crashed in the Iraqi desert.

Damn it. He had no say over his life anymore. His career was in the hands of his commanders. How long was it going to take for them to write him off as officially useless? Waiting for the verdict was like sitting on death row. Before, he could have channeled this restless energy into any one of a dozen adrenaline-pumping activities, all denied him now that he'd lost his equilibrium. All but one.

And now it seemed he couldn't even do that.

"Where are you going?" Grady asked as Cole strode by him.

"What are you, my fucking nursemaid?" Cole kept walking, picking up speed as he cleared the doors.

Grady kept pace with him. "If it's your career you're worried about, Jackson, don't. Even if you did break formation out there, you saved lives. The Air Force will take that into consideration. New orders will come through. You're too valuable an asset for them to—"

"Valuable?" Cole stopped and rounded on him, getting in his face. "As what? They need me to sit behind a desk and push papers? I'd rather take a discharge and sell pencils on a street corner."

"You have twelve years of outstanding service, Major," Grady barked. "You want to throw away a good career feeling sorry for yourself, or are you going to suck it up and do whatever it takes to retire with honor?"

Cole drew in a deep breath. Grady was right. He was losing it. He'd wanted to spend a week partying hard to forget everything for a while. But instead of sin city, this town, surrounded by nothing but desert, seemed like some Twilight Zone limbo land. A kind of weird purgatory where he could only wait around for someone else to decide his future.

With a quick nod, he met Grady's gaze. "I'm going to sleep it off."

"You do that. Come out to the base tomorrow. Hughes has cooked up something brutal to pay McCabe back for her birthday stripper. You gotta see it."

Hughes and McCabe and their practical jokes brought back memories of good times. Cole tried to smile. "I'll be there." He shook hands with Grady and headed up to his room.

Sleep was out, so he showered, and then sat leaning against the headboard and stared at the silent images on the TV, his mind haunted with thoughts of driving out to Nellis tomorrow.

Like a coward, he'd been avoiding the base. Avoiding

the smell of jet fuel, the sleek fuselage of an F-22, the beauty of a Raptor taking off into the blue. All the things that reminded him he'd never fly again. Never feel the thrill of a rocket firing at his back and the pull of G-forces on his body. Of flying faster than the speed of sound and taking his jet so high he could almost see outer space.

But Grady was right. He needed to suck it up and get over it. As his eyes closed, his last thought was of Jordan, how she'd looked when she emerged from the bedroom and seen him playing Gin with her mom. Something in that look had nagged at him.

In the middle of the night, Cole awoke with a painful hard-on and the remnants of an X-rated dream swirling around in his mind. He'd been dreaming of Jordan, clasped tight in his arms in this bed, the sheets rumpled around him as he pumped into her. How was he going to get over this fixation he had for her?

He shoved out of bed, took an ice-cold shower and then shaved. As he stared at the scars on his lower jaw and neck, the first part of his dream clicked into his memory. The part before it turned sexual.

He'd been in Jordan's apartment, cooking for her. She'd been sitting on the counter beside him, more rested than he'd last seen her. And he'd felt…good being able to help. He'd told her he admired her strength to endure her mom's illness, and her determination to better her situation.

And she'd smiled and cupped his face and kissed down his scarred neck.

It hit him all of a sudden: last night was the first night in months that he hadn't woken in a cold sweat from his usual nightmare.

AN HOUR LATER, Cole rolled to a stop at the gate to Nellis and showed the guard his ID. He noticed a red convertible with two women pull up behind him. Dark curls blowing behind the wheel and silky blond hair as long as your arm blowing on the other side. The guard saluted and waved Cole through.

As he watched in his rearview mirror, a female officer stepped out of the guardhouse and spoke with the ladies in the convertible, pointing in the direction of the air combat command buildings. What was that all about?

Shrugging it off, Cole drove around base housing, past the commissary and officers' quarters out to the aircraft hangars. Nellis Air Force Base. Home of the Thunderbirds and the Air Base Defense School. They'd had some good times in Vegas on the weekends back then, and Cole suddenly longed for those uncomplicated days when he'd believed a world of thrills and adventure awaited him after graduation.

With the exception of the newer F-22, everything looked the same as when he'd trained here. C-17s and C-130s sat next to Raptors on the airstrip, and a couple of F-15s screamed overhead as he parked in front of the instructors' buildings.

Hard to believe McCabe and Hughes were air combat instructors here.

Would he have been happy instructing rookie pilots

in air combat? He'd never know. Instructors had to be able to fly.

As he kicked the bike stand down and swung his leg over, Colonel Hogue, 99th Air Base Wing Vice Commander, stepped over to greet him.

Cole stood at attention and saluted.

The colonel returned the salute. "Good morning, Major."

"Good morning, sir." He hadn't expected to be met by the commander. Maybe he should have worn his uniform.

Assessing eyes searched Cole's. "How have you been feeling, Major?"

"Good. Thank you, sir." Was this an official meeting? "I'm more than ready to return to duty, sir."

Just as the colonel nodded, the convertible with the two knockouts pulled up behind Cole's bike, and one lady passenger called out, "Which way to Captain McCabe's office please?"

The colonel scowled, and Cole raised his brows. He was beginning to have an idea about Hughes's prank.

Colonel Hogue answered, "The next building over, down the hall, third door on the right."

"Okay, thanks." The women smiled and blew kisses as they pulled away and parked their car in front of the next building.

"I'd like to know what the hell is going on around here," the colonel grumbled.

Cole kept his mouth strategically shut.

"Well, as you were, Major."

They saluted and Cole strode to the next building and

followed the women to McCabe's office. Both were long-legged beauties, the blonde in tight jeans and a cropped shirt with a tattoo on the small of her back. The brunette wore a miniskirt and a halter top with no bra. And those tanned legs didn't stop. Oh, this was going to be fun to watch.

At McCabe's door, a tall, sleek redhead was just leaving as the other two went in. She eyed Cole up and down with a Mona Lisa smile as she sauntered past him.

McCabe's door was open, so Cole stayed in the doorway, leaned against the frame and folded his arms. Then he grinned.

The two women stood on either side of McCabe, who sat in his chair behind his desk. Pinned in. The poor guy wore a strained smile, his gaze locked on the leggy brunette. The other lady—the one in the miniskirt—hopped up onto the desk next to him, crossed her legs and leaned sideways until her chest was at McCabe's eye level. His gaze shifted to the magnificent cleavage in front of him. His mouth tightened and he swallowed.

"But Mitch," miniskirt said. "I brought Meagan all the way out here to meet you. I was hoping you two might hit it off. Maybe we'd make it a threesome tonight."

A low groan sounded from Mitch's throat. "Baby, make that offer again in a few weeks."

Cole jumped at a hard slap to his back. "How's it going, Jackson?" Hughes stood behind his right shoulder, a wide grin on her face and a sparkle of mischief in her eyes as she stared at McCabe.

McCabe looked up and caught sight of Cole and Hughes. Immediately the misery in his expression changed to wicked amusement. "Ladies, here's someone who's available and looking for companionship. Major Colton Jackson, war hero, just back from Iraq."

THE LADIES turned to look at Cole, their makeup flawless, their lips pouty. Captain Alexandria Hughes had never figured out that whole pout-and-sulk thing that most women used to wrap a man around their finger. It always seemed so artificial. But guys fell for it every time. Most guys anyway. It never seemed to faze Mitch McCabe. But this prank had him on edge. Satisfaction welled in her chest.

Until now, Alex had been enjoying Mitch's misery from afar, listening to reports from the women who'd been streaming in since yesterday afternoon. She must have called almost two dozen of Mitch's ex-lovers yesterday morning. Many still stationed here at Nellis had willingly gone all-in on the prank, and called more women they knew Mitch had slept with.

These two made six who'd shown up so far.

"No hero, just doing my job." Cole gave the women a lazy salute from the doorway.

"Jackson, this is Cynthia and…" McCabe's voice trailed off.

"Meagan," the other woman supplied with a tinge of irritation in her voice.

Cole pushed off the door frame and extended his right hand. "Nice to meet you, ladies."

The women shook his hand, and then glanced at Alex as if asking her permission to take Mitch's offer of Cole.

Alex shrugged. What did she care? Their work was done here.

They each bent over to give McCabe long, sultry kisses on the mouth, and then the brunette grabbed a pen off the desk. "I have to be at work in half an hour, but I'll be home tonight." She took Cole's hand and wrote a phone number on his palm. With a wink to him, she followed her friend out.

While Cole's attention was on the departing women, McCabe scowled and ran a hand through his hair. He probably thought no one was watching him, but Alex saw it.

"What's the matter, McCabe?" she asked as she sauntered into his office. "Not *up* for a threesome tonight?"

McCabe raised a brow and leaned back in his chair, locking his hands behind his head. "Why? You wanted to watch?"

Alex scrunched up her face in disgust. "Rather watch training vids." The truth was, and a tinge of pain sliced through her at the acknowledgment, she was sick of knowing about McCabe's escapades with women.

"You still need training vids on sex?"

"You offering to let me borrow yours?"

McCabe's grin widened and he rocked forward in his chair. "You need them to get off?"

"Oh, I think you're going to need them more than me for the next twenty-eight days."

"At least I have a reason. What's your excuse?"

Alex folded her arms and shrugged. "It's hard getting a date when I hang out with you all the time."

McCabe nodded his understanding. "Guys do tend to feel inadequate around me."

"Hey," Jackson cut in. He'd taken a seat, his gaze shifting back and forth between Mitch and her as if he were watching a tennis match.

"Present company excluded." McCabe glanced at Jackson, then his attention went right back to Alex. "But are you sure I'm the reason you can't get a date?"

If only he knew… Hughes raised one brow. "I did just fine in D.C."

"Those boys in Washington are a bunch of pussies. Every damn one of them has a screw loose."

Alex forced a contented smile. "Some screw loose, and others do it nice and tight." Wasn't that a joke? Though she'd come close to getting some a couple of times, she hadn't had a man in her bed in years. How sad was that?

McCabe sighed. "How many more are going to show up? And I need my cell phone back, by the way."

"All I can say for sure is—" Alex grabbed his phone out of her pocket and tossed it to him "—I had no idea you'd pissed off so many women, McCabe."

He caught the phone, slid it open, and started pressing buttons. "Should've put a lock on this thing," he mumbled.

"Yeah, maybe you should put a lock on your zipper while you're at it."

7

JORDAN PRACTICALLY ran to the employees' dressing room Friday night. Ten o'clock already. The casino floor was so busy she'd barely been able to get away for this quick personal break.

She'd taken her last final exam Thursday morning and the professors were supposed to have posted grades on the university's Web site sometime today. She'd asked a classmate to send a text message to her cell phone when the results were up.

Her nerves a scattered mess, Jordan shifted her weight from one heel to the other, bouncing in impatience as she messed up the combination on her locker three times. Finally she yanked the door open, grabbed her cell out of her purse and checked her messages. Mrs. S had sent her usual mother-sleeping-all's-well note.

"Where's the fire, hon?" Sherri asked, sauntering into the dressing room.

"I'm checking my text messages. I was hoping—"

"Oh, that's right. Your finals."

Jordan nodded as the next message appeared on her screen. "Here it is."

Sherri leaned in to peer over her shoulder. "You aced them all, girl!" She put an arm around Jordan. "I knew you were worrying for nothing."

Sherri's words sounded far away. Jordan dragged in a ragged breath. The text message blurred as reality sank in.

It was over. Jordan went back to work in an endorphin-induced euphoria. It was over. The past few years of burning the candle at both ends had finally paid off. Her thoughts flashed from walking across the stage next weekend and accepting her diploma, to hoping Mom was lucid when she told her, to wanting to celebrate with a pint of Ben and Jerry's.

The ice cream made her think of Cole. She'd caught herself thinking about him way too much since he'd left Tuesday evening.

"Girl, I'm outta here." Sherri dropped her tray of unsold cards at the Keno window. "My babysitter called. The kid just threw up." Bending close, she pecked Jordan's cheek. "Congrats, again, Ms. Brainiac. Go celebrate those grades!" She darted out the door before Jordan could respond.

Jordan slowly made her way to the dressing room and changed out of her uniform. She wrapped her arms around herself and looked around. Employees were coming and going as they did every night at shift change. It seemed weird to think she might not be working here soon. This job had been her savior after Ian left her with no money and behind in the rent. But she'd always planned for it to be temporary. And yet, now she felt nervous. What if she'd spent all these years earning this degree and still couldn't find a job? Or what if she found a job and couldn't cut it?

Come on, Jordan. You did it! She should celebrate. But it was hard to have fun alone. Her mom would be proud— that is, if she remembered who her daughter was.

A hollow sense of loneliness rolled over her.

She wondered… No, Cole had probably already left town. He'd said he was just here for a week, and she hadn't seen him around the casino since she'd returned from her days off. She should have thanked him. Should have told him how much he'd helped her Tuesday. He'd gone above and beyond, and she'd been too proud to appreciate it.

Instead of leaving the back way, Jordan wandered into the casino. She wasn't ready to go home yet. Maybe she'd have one of those huge frozen drinks with an umbrella in it. Why not? She wasn't driving. And Mom usually slept through the night if Mrs. Simco remembered to give her the bedtime meds.

Decided, Jordan headed for the Centrifuge. As she approached the counter she froze in her tracks.

Cole.

He sat three stools down, his head turned away from her. Alone. His fingers tipped a tumbler of light gold liquid back and forth, and he rubbed the knuckles of his other hand across his mouth.

She closed her eyes.

When she opened them, he was staring at her.

His gaze seemed to echo the loneliness and need inside her.

She slid onto the stool beside him. "I—I thought you'd left town."

He blinked and dropped his gaze to her mouth, then returned to her eyes. "Checking out tomorrow."

His voice was raspy. His posture tense. Did he want to be left alone? But he was leaving in the morning. She'd never see him again after tonight. "I wanted to celebrate. Maybe I could buy you a drink?"

Idiot. He already had a drink.

"Celebrate?"

She swallowed, clenched her fists around her backpack strap. "I aced my finals, and I wanted to thank—"

"I never doubted you could do whatever you set your mind to." He lifted his hand and softly touched her cheek. "Be with me tonight, Jordan."

Her stomach contracted. Every cell in her body yearned for him. Common sense, caution, none of that mattered now. He'd be gone tomorrow.

She took his hand and headed for the bar's exit, tugging him after her. He hesitated only long enough to toss a couple of bills next to his drink.

The bank of elevators seemed miles away, and the wait for one eternal. Eventually a ding announced the arrival of the elevator, but it took forever for it to open. Cole's fingers entwined with hers and tightened.

The doors had barely swooshed shut before she turned and covered his lips with hers, shoving him against the wall. He clutched her waist and took control of the kiss, taking her desire and returning it. As his hands moved up to the sides of her breasts, he moaned into her mouth. "I haven't stopped thinking about you all week."

"I've been thinking about you, too." She kissed each corner of his mouth.

"I needed to be with you again," he said, pressing his open mouth to her neck. "I never thought I'd need someone, never expected to feel this way."

A bittersweet joy ramped up the emotions bombarding her. She hitched a leg around his hip and pressed herself against the rigid length in his jeans.

A soft bell chimed and the door slid open. Still moving his mouth sensually over hers, Cole grasped her bottom and lifted her against him. She tightened her legs around his hip and he staggered out of the elevator and down the hall.

At the door to his hotel room, he had to set her down to fish for his key card, but his mouth still moved over hers, hot and demanding. He'd unleashed the dangerous current of emotions she'd sensed lay just beneath his surface.

After the third try getting the door open, he pulled back to watch what he was doing and Jordan blinked away the haze of lust. How had this happened? In an instant he'd convinced her to be with him again.

No. She'd wanted this. Had hoped for this even before she'd seen him in the bar. Before she knew he'd be checking out in the morning. Her mouth laid claim to his neck, inhaling his cologne as he tried to swipe his card. Tomorrow, she'd return to her sensible self and her lonely life. But tonight, she'd abandon responsibility for just a little while. For one last time.

"Jordan." He groaned and she looked down. His hand shook.

Something primitive stirred. She'd made him tremble. She began unbuttoning his shirt while he opened the door. He took her mouth again and walked her backward inside. There were no words, just an urgency that quivered between them. Faster than she would have believed herself capable of, she pulled at his belt, unbuckled it and unzipped him.

The door closed, engulfing them in darkness. He made an impatient sound and she heard him fumbling for the light switch.

An insane urge to giggle rose up, to arch her back and throw her hands in the air and cry out in delicious freedom. Freedom from the restrictions she'd set for herself six long years ago.

The overhead light snapped on. Cole framed her face with his palms and dipped his head to resume the kiss. She could taste the bite of the Cuervo Gold and his raw hunger. Both fed her appetite for him. His hands slid to her shoulders and around her back, edging up under her T-shirt. "Take it off," he mumbled against her lips.

While she jerked her shirt over her head and flung it onto the dresser, he grabbed a condom packet from his jeans, then tossed them aside and pulled her back into his arms. His lips traveled down her jaw to her collarbone, nuzzling down to the edge of her bra. With a hoarse moan, he tugged it down, lifted her breasts, and mouthed one nipple, suckling hard.

Jordan clutched his head. Too much. Too many sensations at once. Sharp aches at her core. Stinging, swelling clit. Liquid desire flooding her passage. He moved to the other nipple and drew it into his mouth, teasing it with his tongue.

The room tumbled and she closed her eyes as he picked her up and carried her to the bed. She lay back, stretching like a cat as his hands fumbled with her jeans. Cool air hit her hips and legs as he slid them and her panties down to her ankles. Another grunt of impatience as her sneakers and socks came off, along with her jeans. Her bare feet were caught in warm hands and placed flat on the mattress so that her knees bent and she let her thighs fall open. She rubbed her aching nipples, wet from his mouth.

"Oh, man," he rasped. "Do that again."

She opened her eyes and rose up on her elbows. He was staring at her hands as they cupped her breasts.

Their gazes met and she began caressing herself and lightly pinching her nipples. She should be self-conscious, embarrassed. But she loved how his lids drooped as he watched and his eyes turned all hazy.

He moaned. "You're so beautiful." Still watching her, he wrenched off his shirt and briefs and for the first time she saw the scars that covered his right side. But even they couldn't detract from the breadth of his shoulders and his muscled torso. His chest was the perfect combination of dark hair, small, tight nipples and rock-like abs. Her stare wandered down to his strong erection and his large, muscled thighs.

He raised a knee onto the bed, crawled up to settle

between her legs, and caressed the back of one hand along the inside of her thigh. "I've been dreaming of this since that night in the desert." Slowly, he lowered his head and slid his tongue into her entrance.

She cried out and her hips lifted off the bed.

His teeth lightly scraped as he sucked and licked. He took his time, pleasuring her with patient thoroughness until he reached her clit. His tongue teased and his lips caressed until Jordan was a whimpering, wiggling mess. But he allowed no resistance. He clamped one hand around her thigh to hold her open and nuzzled in deeper, using his fingers inside her.

Need spiraled, the pressure built, swirling into a hurricane of sensation as his mouth and tongue and fingers worked in her, around her. Her back arched off the bed and she screamed his name as white-hot, blinding pleasure burst from the inside out.

Before she could recover he moved over her and pushed inside. Her body adjusted to the length of him as he filled her completely. Another round of spasms shot through her as he pulled out and thrust again, then lowered to his elbows above her, his hard chest hot against her breasts.

"Jordan." His face was tense, but his eyes were warm, filled with wonder. "I don't want to go tomorrow. I don't want to leave…you." He began to move.

His words overwhelmed her. Too many feelings she'd suppressed for too long swirled around, confusing her. She combed a dark strand back from his forehead and ran her fingers through his hair, then rose up to kiss him.

Wrapping her arms around his neck, she clung to his bunching shoulders as he pumped inside her with deep, driving motions. "I love being inside you." He clamped his jaw shut, wrapped his arms beneath her back and his thrusts got harder, faster, until he drove into her one last time. His eyes squeezed closed, he shuddered, tense and straining. Then he collapsed beside her.

They lay there a long time, damp, sweaty, till their breathing calmed and bodies relaxed. Tentacles of a deep languor pulled at Jordan's body and spirit. But she awakened when she felt Cole get up. She heard him pad to the bathroom and then heard water filling the tub.

He came back to the bed and unhooked her bra and slipped it off. With ease he carried her to the bathroom, lowered her into the hot water, and then stepped in, facing her.

As he sat, he lifted her foot and began massaging her instep with both his thumbs. Jordan moaned and leaned her head back against the rim. Heaven. His large hands wrapped around her foot, strong, and yet gentle, soothing.

"I'm sorry. Maybe you wanted to go out to celebrate?" He cupped her heel in one hand and squeezed, while his other thumb kneaded into the ball of her foot.

"No. This is amazing." With her eyes still closed, she smiled.

He lowered her foot and took the other one, massaging it with the same expertise.

When the silence went on too long, she opened her

eyes, lifted her head and looked at him. Simmering chocolate-brown eyes pierced her. "What?"

"How'd you end up in Vegas?"

She stilled. Why talk about her past with him? This was supposed to be a one-night fling. "How do you know I haven't lived here all my life?"

His brows drew together. "Your mom mentioned a few things."

Jordan pulled her foot from his grasp and drew her knees up, hugging them to her. Talk about a mood killer. Who knows what else her mom had told him?

"Tell me." He reached across and cupped her face, caressing her cheek with his thumb.

Oh, what did it matter? Meeting his gaze, she drew in a deep breath. "My story is disgustingly unoriginal. Girl meets boy. Boy seduces girl into running off to Vegas. Boy takes off and leaves girl stranded."

He dropped his hand. "I want to find the bastard and maim him."

"It was so long ago. He doesn't matter anymore."

"He hurt you."

He said it so tenderly. Suddenly her eyes stung with unshed tears. A protective armor seemed to fall away, letting feelings flood in. She realized she'd had to be strong for so long she'd never allowed herself to acknowledge the pain. There hadn't been time to grieve. Only survive.

"Do you…do you still love him?" His voice, was low, hesitant.

"No." She pulled from his grasp and moved to kneel

between his thighs. Water sloshed and splashed around them as she placed her palm on his cheek and lightly touched her lips to his. "I just haven't let myself feel anything since then. But I can let the hurt go now." She pressed gentle kisses on his nose and eyes and then moved to his right temple and down his scarred neck. "I don't want to be closed off from my feelings anymore."

His arms came round her and brought her to him. "You're amazing." He moved her hair off her shoulder and kissed her there.

"Have you ever…thought you were in love?"

He shook his head. "I've always wanted more out of life than a mortgage and two-point-five kids."

"Did you always know you wanted to be a fighter pilot?"

He grinned. "No, I, of course, wanted to be an astronaut. I used to want to be the first man to walk on Mars."

"Wow, big dream." She raised her brows.

He shrugged. "It didn't seem out of reach. My dad always talked about the day Neil Armstrong first walked on the moon. How amazing it was. When I was ten, he took us to watch the space shuttle *Atlantis* launch from Kennedy Space Center. Skipped school to do it." His gaze wandered to the ceiling and he leaned his head back against the shower tiles. "We drove all night and watched the sun come up."

He was quiet a moment as if remembering, then lifted his head and looked at her again. "After that I read all about the Galileo probe, and tracked it for years thinking someday I'd go to Jupiter, too."

"They have a probe that went all the way to Jupiter?" She turned and sat between his raised knees, leaning back against his chest.

"Yeah. Took six years." He picked up the soap and rubbed it between his palms. "It witnessed a comet crash into Jupiter in '94, orbited it thirty-five times and sent back over fourteen thousand images before it disintegrated in Jupiter's atmosphere in 2003."

In 2003. Seemed like a lifetime ago. She'd graduated high school that May and run off with Ian.

"So, you joined the Air Force to be an astronaut?"

He nodded and his soapy hands cupped her breasts and began caressing them with a slow thoroughness. Jordan moaned.

"That was the plan."

"And you love being a fighter pilot?"

"Oh, yeah. There's no other rush like flying faster than the speed of sound. Went right into the Air Force Academy out of high school. Went to flight school at Randolph in San Antonio, and then trained at Nellis before I was deployed to the Middle East."

She turned in his embrace and raised her fingers to the scars along his shoulder.

"Tell me how it happened." She felt his body stiffen and feared she'd destroyed the moment.

With slippery hands, he lifted her onto his lap and cradled her in his arms. "I was assigned to a special tactics squadron. Our mission was to fly in undetected and establish an assault zone." He was silent for a moment and stared across the bathroom.

"It was my own fault. I got too cocky. Flew in low to draw attention away from ground forces—against orders."

She leaned her head back to look at him. "Did it work?"

He grinned. "Of course." His thumb caressed the side of her breast. "But the insurgents had a missile launcher and I got hit. Still received a letter of reprimand."

"You could have been killed." The thought caused a horrifying lump in her throat.

He shook his head. "I ejected in time."

"But what if you hadn't? What if you'd been knocked unconscious? Or been taken prisoner?"

He shrugged. "I'd rather risk it than live life in half measures. If I had it to do over, I'd—" He stopped. "Damn."

"What is it?"

His arms tightened around her. "I've been pissed at myself for being such a hothead, for ruining my career. But—" he shook his head "—if I had it to do over, I know I'd do the same thing. Every time. Even if it meant losing everything, I wouldn't change what I did."

"That's where we're different. I'd give anything for a do-over. Not for myself, but because I hurt my mom so much by running away."

He squeezed her to him and she wrapped her arms around his neck and pressed her cheek to his shoulder. "I'm sure she understood and forgave you."

Emotions she'd never wanted welled up, an awareness that this experience with him was something more than just sex.

On his right arm, just below his shoulder were the remnants of a tattoo. It looked like a drawing that had been half erased. The rest was all puckered new skin. She traced a finger around it and his gaze followed hers.

"It's a red-tailed hawk," he said softly. "A raptor. It's the name for—"

"—the F-22, I know."

She looked up and their gazes met.

"I figured I'd get another one on my left arm sometime." He brushed the damp hair off her shoulder and slid his hand around her nape, bringing her mouth to his so sweetly, so gently.

With her defenses down, every emotion seemed intensified, every sensation sacred. He'd leave in the morning and she'd never see him again. She wanted to remember this night forever, the intimacy of her breasts pressed to his chest, the sanctuary in his arms, and the possession in his touch as his hands ran down her back.

His kiss enveloped her, surrounding her in a cocoon of protective warmth. He tangled his fingers in her hair as his other hand slid down the column of her throat to her breast and squeezed and played with the nipple. She could feel his erection hard against her stomach.

With one arm around her waist, the other beneath her bottom, he lifted her as she straddled his lap. "I wanted to go slow the next time, but…" With a groan he gripped her hips and pushed her down over his hard length. His head thrown back, his eyes closed, he moved inside her.

Jordan gripped the rim of the tub behind his shoulders and rocked her hips to create a rising friction.

He groaned her name. His Adam's apple bobbed as he swallowed and she lowered her mouth to the tendons at the junction of his neck and shoulder, nipping her way up his scars to his earlobe.

He slid his hand between them and began to stroke her.

Jordan cried out as he brought her to a writhing, sobbing pleasure. Water sloshed over the edge of the tub as her movements became more frenzied, but she didn't care. With every rise and fall of her hips she felt her passage stretch for him, felt him so deep inside her, filling her. The thought sent her over the edge. She gripped his shoulders as wave after wave rocked her.

He bent his knees and curled his fingers into her waist as his hips rose and he spent himself inside her.

Falling limp against him, she laid her head on his shoulder, satiated as she'd never been before. Lazily, she listened to his breathing return to normal and knew she'd never forget this night, this experience, this man. Not for as long as she lived. She'd be an old lady, a grandmother, a great-grandmother, and she'd still recall this night.

His chest rose as he drew in a deep breath and sat up. "Jordan. I didn't— Are you…protected?"

Omigosh. She wasn't. How could she have ever expected this? For a panicked moment, Jordan drew a complete blank as she tried to remember where she was in her cycle. Think, Jordan. This was the third week of May. Memory returned. She should be safe.

"Um…no, but, it should be okay," she said with more confidence than she felt. Wouldn't that be the stupidest thing she'd ever done? Just as she was getting her life straight.

"Are you sure? I can't believe I didn't even think about it. Just so you know, I've had all the tests."

She nodded, but she wanted to slap herself. "I've never needed to." Before now. She'd always insisted Ian wear a condom. How *could* she have been so irresponsible this time?

"Okay." He let out a deep breath. "But you promise you'll contact me if…I'll leave my contact info, all right?" He stood, water sluicing down his skin, and bent to give her a hand. "You hungry?"

Her stomach growled, but the reality of her situation hit her hard. Did he think she was trying to trap him? He'd made it clear from the beginning he wasn't the home-and-hearth kind of guy. She had to get to her place, be with her mom. She shouldn't have stayed this late. What would Mrs. Simco say?

"No, I should go." Shoving her hair out of her face, she tried to stand on her own, but he clasped her elbows and lifted her against him, skin to skin. Their gazes locked. Then he stepped out and grabbed a thick, fluffy robe from a hook and draped it around her shoulders.

The spell of the evening had definitely been broken.

As she pushed her arms through the sleeves, he wrapped a towel around his waist and padded into the suite. "Are you sure I can't get you something?" he called to her.

Jordan closed her eyes. He was trying to fill the

awkward silence. One would think she'd have learned by now that acting irresponsibly always had its consequences.

She forced herself to leave the bathroom and started gathering her clothes and backpack. "The lady who watches my mother will be wondering what happened to me."

"Oh, right. Of course." Cole grabbed her T-shirt and handed it to her. "So, your mom can't stay alone at all?"

"No, not anymore." She stood clutching the robe together at her neck with her clothes bunched in front of her. She wanted to retreat to the bathroom to dress, but it seemed kind of silly after what they'd done together. For a moment she let herself relive the feel of his mouth on her, of his hard body against her, of him coming inside her. It seemed strange to think she'd never see him again after tonight.

"It's Alzheimer's, right? Who watches her? You have a nurse?"

"No, right now, it's a neighbor of mine, Mrs. Simco. She's really good with her."

He nodded, meeting her gaze without pity this time. "How long has she been sick?" Casually, he dropped his towel and pulled some clean briefs from a drawer.

"It's been about three years since we noticed the initial symptoms." Jordan was still standing with her clothes in her arms. She dropped everything on the bed and started dressing. "At first, she forgot normal things. Like we all do sometimes. Certain words, or where she'd put her glasses." She remembered those early days, when her mom would call from Iowa, and Jordan would make a joke about Alzheimer's. "Then one day I called home, and she was crying and scared. She'd been late for work because she couldn't remember how to get to the diner. That's when she knew something was wrong. She'd worked at that diner almost twenty years."

"I can't imagine what she's been through. What you've both been through." While she talked, he'd pulled on the same jeans and shirt he'd worn earlier.

Jordan nodded. No one could unless they'd lived it.

"I'll give you a ride." He sat on the edge of the bed and tugged on his boots.

"Oh, no. That's okay." She fumbled in her backpack for her brush and started trying to tame her hair.

He looked up at her, his jaw set. "It's four in the morning. I'm taking you home."

Stepping into her sneakers, she wrestled her hair into a ponytail. "Okay."

He escorted her downstairs, and into the parking garage, and loaned her his jacket again before getting on his bike and taking her home. After he walked her to her apartment door, he took her by the shoulders and gave her a slow lingering kiss.

Oh, God, she wished the kiss would go on forever. Any day his orders would come through and he'd be shipped back to Iraq. But she wouldn't regret this night. He'd helped her feel alive again. And not so afraid of her wild side.

But what about him? He was a daredevil fighter pilot. What if something happened to him again?

The thought of him being killed brought a chill to her

chest. She tore her mouth from his and hugged him tightly around the neck. "Be careful, Cole." Before she could burst into tears in front of him, she gave him one last quick squeeze, then rushed inside and shut the door.

She was still wearing his jacket.

BY SUNUP Cole was speeding down Highway 92 halfway to Phoenix. After he'd dropped Jordan off, he'd packed and checked out, unable to stay in that room a minute longer.

Sand stung his face as Cole roared down the dark, deserted road. The constant grit in his eyes reminded him of the sandstorms that had sometimes grounded his squadron in Iraq.

Still, this desert could never resemble the vast ocean of barren land that was the Sandbox. It was good to be home. Here you drew a breath and smelled clean air, mostly. There you smelled burning oil or human decay. And the oppressive sense of hopelessness.

Although, right now, he'd give anything to be able to return to combat.

Maybe if he'd known he was shipping out for another tour of duty, then this trip to Vegas would have been just like any other leave. Fast and fun. He wouldn't have gotten so attached to one woman just because he had sex with her. That had to be what it was, right?

He'd never, ever had a beautiful, naked woman in his arms and wanted to…talk. And he'd certainly never felt as if he might want to stay and see where the relationship might—wait a minute. He screeched to a stop and pulled off onto the shoulder of the highway. Had he just used the word *relationship?* He closed his eyes and gritted his teeth. That's enough of this mushy thinking, Jackson. It was a fling. It was fun.

It was over.

He could always buy a new leather jacket.

8

GENERAL James Jackson, retired USAF, Vietnam veteran and descendant of Thomas "Stonewall" Jackson, answered the door in a worn robe over his skivvies. "Colton."

Cole smiled as his father stepped forward and gripped his right hand, slapping him on the back with the left.

"We weren't expecting you so early." General Jackson shut the door behind Cole. "I just brewed some coffee."

Cole's chest tightened as his father led the way into the kitchen. Everything looked the same. He'd been thirteen when his dad had retired from the Air Force and taken a job in Phoenix. Being back in this house brought back a lot of memories.

Nothing had changed in the twelve years since he'd left. Including the sight of his mom standing at the stove, cooking bacon and eggs. "Who was it, Jim?" She turned and her round face exploded in joy. "Cole!" She dropped her spatula on the counter, wiped her hands on a dishtowel and threw her arms around him. "Honey, you must have driven all night. Sit down and have something to eat."

As he sat and ate, his mother restrained herself with small talk for a few minutes before asking what she really wanted to know. "So, did you have a nice time with your friends in Vegas?"

Vegas. Jordan. In the tub, her slick soft breasts pressed against him. Aw, hell. He shifted in his chair. "Uh, yeah. It was good."

"Your mother was worried." His father put the newspaper down. "I tried to tell her you needed a few days to—" he cleared his throat "—relax before you visited us, but you know your mother."

Cole cringed at the thought of his parents discussing his, er…love life.

"What's important is you're home now." His mom stood and smiled. "I planned a little get-together."

ALL BUT ONE of Cole's siblings lived in Phoenix and his middle brother and sister-in-law were flying in.

Cole barely had time to clean up and take a quick nap before they began filing in. His older brother was lugging in baby gear, and kids trailed after him. His wife was nagging the poor guy before they even made it into the living room.

Cole's older sister, who was divorced with two sullen teens, spent the afternoon griping about her ungrateful brats and how she never had any time to herself.

This was just what Cole needed. Reality check 101.

His middle brother had married a little over a year ago, and his other sister had brought along her latest and they couldn't seem to keep their eyes off each other.

Cole lagged behind his family, watching as they settled at the big dining-room table. His mother was smiling, happy to have all her kids and grandkids around, though she kept sneaking worried glances at him. They were all here to see him, and yet, as they discussed their children and their schedules and lives, he felt like the odd man out. An outsider. Alone.

In the years he'd been overseas, his brothers and sisters had...gotten old. Given up. Just like Dad.

His old man had only been twenty-two when he'd married Mom. He'd had four kids by the time he was Cole's age. All those years. Taking desk jobs to get promotions, turning down flying assignments to stay home for kids' birthdays and school plays. He could have gone into the space program and been one of the first men to walk on the moon if he hadn't married.

Nothing had ever been said directly, only hinted at in rare unguarded moments—usually while watching space-shuttle launches on TV, which Dad never missed. But Cole figured his father must lie in bed at night wishing he'd done things differently.

He had to regret his ordinary life. The bills, the mortgages, the burdens he'd taken on at such a young age. He must think about how exciting his life could've been if he hadn't been tied down by a wife and five kids. The things he could have seen and done, the impact he could have made on the world. He had to have wanted just to take off, chuck it all, and live his own life. Hell, he probably still did.

By ten o'clock that night, all of Cole's brothers and

sisters had left, except for his oldest brother, who was hauling his third load of kids' paraphernalia out to a worn minivan with a sliding door that stuck. What the hell had happened to that 'Vette his brother had always wanted?

Cole couldn't take anymore. The evening was still young and he itched to get out for a beer and some pool. Hell, he'd settle for a video arcade. He stopped his brother as he came back inside. "Hey, Kenny. How about going out for a beer?"

"Oh, uh…" His brother hesitated, and Cole realized the poor sap probably had to get permission. Cole couldn't imagine having to check with someone before every move.

Kenny's wife came up behind them. "You should go, honey."

"But the kids…"

"I manage corporate attorneys all day, I think I can handle the rug rats alone for a while."

Kenny's eyes softened and he put an arm around his wife. "I can't leave Jenny with her asthma so bad." He turned back to Cole. "She gets scared and wants her daddy when she can't breathe."

"Oh, honey." His wife looked at Kenny as if he'd just saved the world from a terrorist attack. Was this the same couple who'd been bickering earlier?

"Cole, if you're anything like your brother—" his sister-in-law turned her attention to him "—you're going to make a great daddy some day." She looked back at her husband and squeezed his waist.

Ignoring the tiny voice in his head that was actually

considering such a thing, Cole bit back a fervent denial. Instead he smiled and shrugged, then waved goodbye as the underpowered minivan squeaked its way down the street.

In a strange mood, Cole headed back inside his parents' house.

He stopped short at the entry to the den. His dad was standing in front of the fireplace holding the framed picture of Cole receiving his Air Force Combat Action Medal.

One of Cole's best days, bar none. His parents had been there, his mother blotting her eyes with a tissue, and if his father's chest had puffed out any further, he'd have been able to float in the Macy's Thanksgiving Day parade.

Feelings surfaced he'd thought were long buried, of relief at finally making his old man proud. As the youngest of five, Cole was definitely an oops baby. His father had made no attempt to hide the fact that Cole was unexpected. And, Cole assumed, unwanted. Even his mom still told stories in an affectionately exasperated voice about his wild ways and all his emergency-room trips, and joked about how she should have stopped at four.

With two older brothers also in the Air Force, getting noticed by his busy father became even more of a challenge. So, no way Cole was not going to join. And he excelled at everything. Trying to show them all what the "wild child" could do, he'd set about breaking records instead of bones, and ended up the top of his class.

Even before 9/11 he'd been eager to be deployed. And then he'd served a tour in Afghanistan with distinction. Cole had reveled at the pride in his father's eyes.

But that pride wasn't there tonight. What Cole saw was worry. His dad had to know the details of why Cole had been shot down. Yet, the old man hadn't said anything in the hospital. Well, his mother had been there then, and Cole had still been recovering.

His dad replaced the photo on the mantel. "You think they'll discharge you?"

"Maybe," Cole answered. "Maybe that'd be for the best."

His father turned and nailed him with an unnerving look. "You think you're too good to serve if you can't fly?"

"No, sir." Cole fought the urge to curl his hands into fists.

"Without the people on the ground, pilots wouldn't be in the air. The man who packs your parachute is just as important as you are."

"I know that."

"Air Force's mission is to fly and fight, and just because you can't be a hotshot anymore doesn't mean there aren't other ways you can serve your country, Colton."

"So I should just give up my dream like you did?" Damn. He hadn't meant to blurt that out. Although maybe it was time to clear the air.

Sparks shot from his father's eyes. "Why don't you request an honorable discharge if that's what you want?"

Cole blew out a deep breath. "I don't know what the hell I want." Or even who he was anymore.

"That's your problem, right there." His father fisted his hands on his hips. "You should talk to someone."

"Like a shrink?" Cole snorted. "I'll be fine."

The old man grunted. "That's what I said when I got home from 'Nam." He walked to the front window and clasped his hands behind his back. "But I wasn't."

"Your mother wouldn't marry me until I got help," his dad continued.

What? Cole had never heard about this.

"And let me tell you, convincing her to give me another chance was harder than talking to that therapist." He shot his son a sly grin. "But nine months after I persuaded her to marry me, Charlotte was born."

There was an image Cole could've done without. "What if you hadn't tried to persuade her?"

His dad turned back to Cole and frowned. "What do you mean?"

"Well, back then it was different. Men were supposed to get married, right? But what if you hadn't? What if you'd followed your dream, instead? If you hadn't been burdened with all of us, you could have done anything."

"Burdened? What are you talking about? What dream?"

"To be an astronaut. To walk on the moon. To have adventures beyond belief."

His father shrugged. "I could've done that, I suppose, if I'd wanted. But I never would've left your Mom for that long, especially not after you kids were born."

Cole nodded. "Exactly. Having a family tied you down. We kept you from your dream."

His dad's forehead wrinkled in confusion. "Where'd you get your intel, Major? I wasn't tied down. I had everything I ever wanted." He stepped closer and held Cole's gaze. "After I made it back from 'Nam, my only dream was to marry my girl and build a home for our family. My mission became all about getting my head straight and loving your mom.

"I loved the Air Force. I loved flying—still do. But it doesn't come close to the thrill of loving my wife."

Like a punch to the gut the truth hit Cole, and a lifetime of beliefs shattered. Reality shifted and the universe seemed to tilt. Dad was gray and balding, with creases of age around his eyes. But Cole could see in those eyes the fervor of the young man he'd once been. That fervor Cole had always interpreted as wanderlust was really just the fire of a man who knew what he wanted and went after it.

Suddenly, Cole envied his father that kind of certainty.

"You okay, son?"

He cleared his throat. "Yes, sir."

His old man stepped close and clasped his shoulder. "I'm going to bed. So think about this. If you still want to join the space program, you don't have to fly a jet to work for NASA." He narrowed his eyes and folded his arms across his chest. "But you do have to have your head on straight."

He dropped his arms and headed for the stairs. "Think about it."

THINK ABOUT IT. Over the next couple of days, thoughts whirled around Cole's head with the velocity of a hurricane. On Monday morning his commander called on his cell to issue new orders. He'd been assigned as an air traffic controller at Lackland Air Force Base in San Antonio. He was to report there in a week. Not bad. He should be happy. But Cole couldn't seem to work up the appropriate enthusiasm.

His father's words kept echoing in his mind. That and the way his brother and sister-in-law had looked at each other as they were leaving Saturday night. Would Cole be happier at his new job if he had Jordan in his bed every night? Relationship as an adventure, not a prison sentence. He tried to wrap his brain around the concept. But he wasn't his dad. Or his brother, for that matter. He just couldn't see himself as the home-and-family type.

Then why did he keep thinking about one gorgeous, hard-working Keno girl? Maybe he *was* becoming a Jordan junkie. What was it about her that was so addictive?

Up in his old room, he lay on the bed with his hands behind his head remembering how Jordan had looked all tousled and sleepy in his hotel room. How she'd kissed her way down his scars, and the look in her eyes as she'd taken him inside her in the tub. The teasing curve to her smile when she'd admitted to liking the way he celebrated her grades.

And yet, it was more the way he felt when he was around her. Or maybe it was about how he felt when she wasn't around. As if something was missing.

Cole sat up. His dad was right. He needed to get his head straight. Maybe seeing her one more time before taking off for Texas would answer all his questions. After being away from her for almost a week, maybe he'd be more objective now. And hey, he needed to get his jacket back.

He hoped McCabe's couch was comfortable.

JORDAN COULDN'T STOP the tears. It was ridiculous, but as soon as the band had started playing "Pomp and Circumstance" the waterworks hit her and she'd had to blink furiously and clench her teeth. At this rate, she'd have no mascara left.

Maybe because she'd missed her high-school graduation ceremony when she ran off with Ian, the ritual today meant so much more. For the first time since she'd been hired, she'd taken a Friday night off from The Grand. And she'd bought a new dress. Yet, it was bittersweet.

She sat with the rest of her graduating class in rows of folding chairs on the convention-center floor, but she kept glancing up into the stands at Mrs. Simco and her mother. As far as Jordan could tell, Mom was doing really well. When they'd parted ways at the convention-center entrance, Tammy had had no idea why she was here, but she'd seemed content enough. And Mrs. Simco had assured Jordan she would take her home if she had any problems.

Since Jordan's last name started with a *B*, it wasn't long before her row stood up to accept their diplomas. Her stomach churned and her nails dug into her palms as she got closer to the stage. It wasn't that she was nervous, it was just that it was a moment to be remembered and she yearned to have someone to share it with who truly understood.

In an instant her name was being called and she was walking across the stage and shaking the dean's hand. Moving her tassel from right to left, she glanced up to where her mother and Mrs. S were standing and caught a flash of something glinting off the dark blue suit of—

It wasn't a suit. It was a uniform. A dress uniform. The medals on his coat reflected the bright lights.

It was Cole.

Jordan's stomach somersaulted and a silly happiness bubbled up. The tears she'd successfully blinked away before were back.

Someone nudged her from behind and she jumped, then realized they were prodding her to get off the stage. Her face heating in embarrassment, she hurried down the steps and filed back into the row of seats. Once she sat down through, she looked into the stands.

He was still there. Not a mirage. Standing ramrod-straight next to her mother, still applauding. Even from such a distance, his stare burned through her. Then he lifted his right hand and saluted her before taking her mom's arm and helping her to sit down and sat beside her.

Jordan blinked away more ridiculous tears and forced herself to sit through the rest of the ceremony. But each time she glanced back, he was still there.

She hadn't expected her mother to last, though, and by the time the students whose last names started with

M were filing on stage, Jordan saw Mrs. Simco and Cole helping her mom up the stairs to the exit. Gratitude was muddled with disappointment. Emotions welled in her throat as she watched them all disappear from the arena.

An hour later, it was finally over and, after ditching the rented gown, she made her way outside, preparing to hail a cab. But there he was. Waiting in the warm night beneath a street lamp across the road. So handsome in his sharply pressed uniform with medals and ribbons pinned down its front.

With the crowd swirling around her, she watched him unobserved for a moment. He'd cut his hair and the short cut combined with his stiff posture screamed *military officer*. So different from the scruffy, jeans-clad bad boy on a motorcycle she'd first met. But the unsmiling intensity of his dark gaze was the same as he scanned the throngs of people exiting the convention center.

She stepped off the curb and crossed the street. He caught sight of her and his eyes widened, then heated as they traveled down her body and back up again. Coming to a stop before him, she shifted her weight from one heel to the next and wiped her damp palms down the fabric of the tight black dress.

When their gazes met again, he smiled. In an instant his face transformed from starkly handsome to boyishly good-looking, and all Jordan could do was stare and try to catch the breath that had left her lungs.

"Hi," he said.

"You came back." What a stupid thing to say. Of course he was here. "Uh, I mean, I thought you were shipping out. Back to Iraq."

He shook his head. "Went to visit my folks in Phoenix."

"Oh." Dozens of thoughts and questions spun around in her mind. Had he come back just for her? Or was he required to be here to await orders? Where was he staying? Was he only here for one night?

"Did you talk to Mrs. Simco? Is my mom okay?"

"I did." He nodded. "And she is." He clasped his hands before him and rocked on his heels.

Jordan found herself leaning forward in anticipation of his next words, but they never came. "So, what are you doing here?"

He shrugged and looked up at the convention center. "Just sightseeing."

Jordan blinked up at him until a smile slowly spread across his face. "I'm here to take you out to dinner, egghead. To celebrate."

"Oh." Here she was, a college graduate, and "oh" seemed to be the sum total of her vocabulary. How embarrassing.

"So." He extended his elbow. "Shall we go?"

There was nothing she wanted more. But first… She opened her purse and pulled her cell phone out.

"Mrs. S said to have a good time and don't come back too early." He grinned, took her hand and curled it around his arm.

Jordan stared at his hand on hers, feeling the warm roughness of it, the promise in his touch, the anticipation tingling from him into her. Then she looked up into his eyes and saw a truth reflected there. He'd come back to Vegas…for her.

9

OBJECTIVITY hit the proverbial fan when Cole saw Jordan again. Meeting her gaze, he felt a jolt shoot through him. Hell, it was as if she saw something in him no one else saw. She looked past the Air Force officer and saw something…more.

Pulling his keys from his pocket, he led her out to the parking lot, but Jordan hesitated beside his Harley, her adorable brows crinkled.

"Um…" She glanced down at her tight black dress and heels.

Cole could've kicked himself. He hadn't thought. Eight hours of planning every last detail for tonight, including enlisting Grady's help for special clearance at Nellis, and he hadn't thought to rent a car. "I'll get us a cab." He turned to head for the street.

"No." She grabbed his arm. "It'll be okay."

"You sure?"

At her nod, he mounted the bike then held out his hand to her.

She hitched up her dress, took his hand, then stepped up on the footrest and swung her leg over.

He gulped. That glimpse of bare thigh beneath her dress turned him on more than the stockings and mini-skirt of her casino uniform. It was going to be an uncomfortable ride.

She leaned close, her hands sliding to clasp around his chest, and nuzzled her nose into his spine.

Cole's insides shook. Having her pressed against him reduced him to a quivering mess. Clenching his fists, he started the engine and pulled out of the lot.

The eight miles from downtown out to the base seemed like eighty-eight with Jordan's hands on him. Thankfully, her fingers didn't stray below his belt. When he pulled up to Nellis's gate, the guard stepped out; Cole showed his ID and Jordan supplied her social security number, her expression doubtful. The guard opened the gate and waved Cole through with a salute.

If Jordan wondered where they were going, she kept it to herself as they circled around the squadron's hangars and headed out to a remote field. He came to a stop just outside the hangar that housed several retired Second World War aircraft, kicked the Harley's stand down, and held out his hand to help Jordan climb off.

She gave him a cautious look, and he couldn't help himself. He smiled, knowing what waited inside. The hangar was dark except for the streetlight at the barbed-wire-topped fence surrounding the base.

"Worried?"

"This isn't exactly what I had in mind when you said 'out to dinner.'" She arched a brow, trying for nonchalance, he guessed, but then ruined the effect by grinning.

She'd pulled her hair up into some fancy style, but the ride had blown it into wild magnificence. She looked so beautiful, so soft and feminine he had to hold himself back not to pull her into his arms.

"Trust me?"

"Yes," she answered without hesitation, as if her simple *yes* held a deeper meaning.

Cole shoved down a lump of emotion and reached into his pants pocket and pressed the button on the garage door opener.

Rumbling and grinding, the hangar door lifted. Cole ducked under and strode in to light the candles and turn on the CD. Pure satisfaction filled him as he heard her soft gasp.

Delmonico's had provided the table setting, but Cole had arranged for a buffet cart to hold his ingredients and a couple of mini propane burners so he could sauté his own shrimp and cook the pasta. He'd hand-selected the prosciutto and asparagus that morning.

His breathing quickened as he returned to Jordan and led her inside the hangar.

"Oh, how beautiful." Her eyes glowed with appreciation as her gaze roamed over the white cloth table set with china, silver, fresh flowers and candles. "Oh, Cole."

So far, so good. She liked.

She cupped a rose from the vase, leaned down and inhaled. "They're gorgeous."

"The lady at the florist's shop said the combination of red and yellow together meant Congratulations."

"Wow." She rounded the table, closed the distance

between them, and planted a quick kiss on his cheek. "You keep surprising me." She held his gaze for a split second while he stood immobilized by the look in her eyes. The same look had been in his sister-in-law's eyes when Kenny had turned down a night of beer and pool. Before Cole could recover, Jordan turned and walked over to the nearest aircraft. "What kind of plane is this?"

"She's a B-24, a Liberator." He followed her over to the plane, lifted his free hand and touched one of the four giant propellers. "Probably flew over most of German-occupied Europe. She had eleven machine guns, and carried an eight-thousand-pound bomb load. Winston Churchill had one of these babies customized for his personal transport."

Her heels clicked on the cement as she walked around the bomber's nose. "Think of all the stories this plane could tell. How many men sacrificed their lives? How many did she bring safely home?" She was almost whispering, a hint of reverence in her voice. He turned and saw her staring up at the glass, front-mounted machine-gunner's cabin. He couldn't take his eyes off her.

"Yeah. I think about that, too. My dad used to tell us about his uncle Joe flying over the Pacific in the Second World War. But he never talks about 'Nam."

She turned her big blue eyes on him. "No matter how worthy the cause is, I imagine war haunts you."

Cole thought of his nightmares and the counselor who'd told him they were nothing to be ashamed of. Here, now, with Jordan, that didn't seem so ridiculous.

With a quick smile he gestured toward the elegant dining table. "Dinner will be served in a few minutes."

She slipped her hand into his and let him lead her to the table. "So, you *are* going to feed me," she said lightly, letting the subject of war go.

His fingers tightened around hers. "Did you ever doubt me?" He pulled out a chair for her.

A pause, then "Not lately."

At her careful choice of words, he raised a brow. "Fair enough."

She sat and snapped open her thick linen napkin, placing it over her lap, then smiled up at him. "I still can't believe you did all this."

Cole shrugged, trying to ignore his pounding heart. "We're celebrating, right?" While soft jazz played, he poured champagne. Then he took off his uniform coat and tie, rolled up his sleeves and began preparing the meal.

She crossed her legs and took a sip of champagne. "Where did you learn to cook?"

"Believe it or not, in Alaska." He explained about the summer he'd spent up there between his junior and senior years with the son of an Air Force buddy of his father's who'd bought a restaurant in Anchorage. Their fathers had flown together in 'Nam. Cole shrugged. "I ended up hanging out in the kitchen."

"So your great-uncle, your father and you—all military pilots? Flying runs in your family?"

"Yep."

"You must love being up there, speeding through the sky."

Damn. His throat tightened. "Yeah."

"Adrenaline junkie, right? Into extreme sports?"

Could he refuse to answer any more questions except his name, rank and serial number? He forced a smile. "You bet. Can't keep me away."

"Being cooped up in the hospital must have been awful for you."

"Oh, I don't know. All those sponge baths..." He wiggled his brows and gave her a pointed look as he glanced at her.

Something—disappointment?—flickered in her eyes before she covered it with a patently fake smile. "Oh, right." She looked away and started swinging her crossed leg.

Mistake. Big mistake. Maybe he should tell her he'd never fly a jet again. Tell her the most exciting thing he'd be doing now was air traffic control. He'd been reduced to a freaking traffic cop.

But bringing up his new assignment might lead to more questions. Questions about their future that he had no answers for. He poured the pasta into the boiling water and turned the shrimp.

From the corner of his eye he could feel her gaze on him. The burners didn't produce as much heat as her stare. "I shouldn't have said that," he said, backtracking. "You were being serious and I was—"

"No, it's fine." Her face glowed softly in the candlelight, but she looked vulnerable now, closed off. Damn it.

Unease shot through his gut as he filled their plates and sat beside her. He lifted his champagne glass with another forced smile. "To an intelligent and beautiful lady," he toasted her. "Congratulations."

Her eyes softened and she picked up her glass and clinked it against his. "Thank you." But she avoided his gaze while she sipped.

Without another word, she picked up her fork and started eating.

He took a bite of shrimp and swallowed. Another moment of awkward silence followed. Somehow he had to regain what had been lost.

"I hated every second in the hospital."

At last, she looked at him. "You don't have to—"

"No, it's okay." He cleared his throat. "I was in the hospital in Germany for about three weeks. Then another three weeks in the States. Followed by a couple of months in rehab."

"But you're back in shape now? Ready for action?" Her mouth curved in a small smile.

Was that a double entendre? Could she be as innocent as her expression seemed? "Yes, ma'am. Ready and willing."

Her eyes flared wide and her cheeks pinked. That started his engines. "How about you? Are you still going to work at The Grand?"

"I can't afford to quit until I have another job lined up." Jordan's eyes lit up. "But I have two interviews next week."

Unreasonable panic stabbed at him. If he'd been released from the hospital just a few weeks later, he might never have met Jordan. "Interviews with whom?"

"One is with a new research development corporation. I'd be a systems programmer. The other is with Nevada Power, supporting their internal e-mail systems.

That one sounds more likely since it's an entry-level position." She pressed her palms to her stomach. "I'm so nervous. I've dreamed of this for so long."

"You'll do great. You've worked hard. I know you'll get everything you wish for."

"Thank you." She smiled at him and held his gaze for a long moment before picking up her fork and taking another bite.

"Where are you staying?"

"I'm crashing at McCabe's for now, the miserable SOB."

"What do you mean? Why is he miserable?" She took a dainty bite, confusion in her big blue eyes.

Oh, hell, she hadn't known the details of the bet. "Never mind. I shouldn't have brought it up."

"No, tell me. You can't leave me hanging."

Shaking his head, knowing he'd probably regret it, he explained the conditions of the bet, and how Hughes had used it to get back at McCabe last week.

"Captain Hughes? Get him back for what?"

"McCabe and Hughes have been pulling practical jokes on each other for years. It all started as a good deed by McCabe."

"A good deed? Captain McCabe?" Her skeptical tone wasn't lost on Cole.

"You have to understand. When Hughes first joined our squadron, the guys treated her differently because she's female. So, naturally he had to do something awful to her, something he would've done to any new cadet, to prove that she was just one of the guys."

"I never thought of it that way." Her voice lowered to a conspiratorial whisper. "What'd he do?"

"He had her arrested for soliciting a prostitute."

"Oh, no!" Jordan's eyes widened.

"The whole thing was staged. She was fine." Leaning close, he added, "She paid him back a few months later."

A wicked grin lit up her beautiful face. "What'd *she* do?"

"Uh, I'll let her tell you about that."

Jordan groaned in frustration. "At least tell me what she did to him last week."

Cole grinned at her enthusiasm. "She must've called every woman McCabe ever sl—dated and invited them all on base to torture him."

Jordan's boisterous laugh was contagious. She brought her napkin up to her mouth, looked at him and broke into laughter again. "I should shake Captain Hughes's hand. See if she wants to have lunch some-time."

"Oh, no, I have a feeling you two getting together might be hazardous to a guy's health. And I gotta live with said guy."

Her smile soared across the table and hit him right in the gut. He watched her finish eating, mesmerized when her lips closed around her fork. She reached up and tucked a strand of hair behind her ear and he envisioned nibbling the tender spot behind her delicate silver earring. The movement also shifted the front of her dress. It came to a V between her breasts, and the rounded flesh peeking out moved with her every breath, enticing him, torturing him.

"So, how long before you have to leave?"

Cole shifted his gaze to her face and blinked. He had to bring his mind back from the brink of his sex-on-the-table fantasy and think about what she'd just asked. "I have to be in San Antonio on Monday."

"This Monday?" She sounded shaken. He'd wanted to do something special for her graduation and see her one more time before heading to Texas. Though he hadn't thought how she might interpret this dinner.

He avoided looking at her as he got to his feet and started clearing dishes. "I should get you home."

"Yeah." Jordan stood, too, grabbing the champagne glasses.

"You don't need to do that, I have a cleaning crew coming in." He took the crystal from her and their hands brushed. Just that small contact made him feel as if the room had become a vacuum and he was without his oxygen. When he looked at her, her lips were parted. Her eyes had darkened to a stormy ocean blue.

Incapable of stopping himself, he leaned in and kissed her, just a feather touch, barely brushing across her mouth. Then he pulled back. He hadn't meant to assume anything tonight. Every muscle tensed, he stood there.

She reached up and ran her hand down his temple and jaw. Her touch left a trail of fire along his skin. Then her hold pulled him toward her and she pressed her lips to his. Soft, open-mouthed, deep.

Cole groaned, wrapping his arms around her, pulling her tightly against him. He wished they could stay here, in their own little world where no one could intrude. In her arms he was sure of himself. He felt as if his life had purpose. Her hands ran under the collar of his shirt, and her stomach pushed against his rock-hard erection. His body screamed for more.

He cupped her bottom and lifted her to the table, shoving silverware and napkins aside as he stepped between her knees. His lips traveled down her soft neck to the hollow of her throat, and farther down, nuzzling as far as the dress would allow, tasting her supple flesh.

"Cole," she moaned his name, and it enflamed his already desperate need. He slid a hand under the hem of her dress, savoring the creamy skin of her thigh.

Without warning she grabbed his hand and pushed him away. "I can't."

His breathing ragged, Cole closed his eyes. His blood pounded. His cock ached. "I didn't expect you—" he gestured to the table behind her "—this, tonight."

"It's not that I don't want to." She slowly slid off the table, adjusting her dress, fidgeting with her hair. Then she drew a deep breath and let it out as if coming to a momentous decision.

Not good.

"It's just better for me if I don't get any more involved." Finally her eyes lifted to meet his gaze. "It'd be more than just a fling then and I can't—"

"I get it." He didn't want that, either. Her life was here, with her mother. His was in Texas. Or wherever the Air Force sent him. He shouldn't have come back here.

But he hadn't been able *not* to come back, to her.

"I loved the dinner." She turned, picked up her

purse and scooted her chair in, then smiled at him again. "You be careful out there, okay?" Her smile was tinged with sadness and something broke inside Cole. This couldn't be the end. A week ago he'd told himself it was over between them. But he'd been fooling himself. Maybe there was a way to work something out. He couldn't think how, still, did that matter right now?

"Can I see you again tomorrow night? We'll walk the strip and see all the stuff tourists come for. I've never done that." He left unspoken, *And I want to see it all with you.*

"I work tomorrow night. All the touristy stuff stops at midnight."

"It doesn't matter. We can get something to eat, walk around, see the hotels. One more night."

It was as if she held his future in her hands. He watched with a plunging gut as she dropped her gaze to the table. She pulled a rose from the vase and began playing with the petals. She was quiet so long he thought maybe he'd missed something she said because of his deaf ear.

Eventually, she lifted her head and pierced him with a determined look. "One more night."

AFTER Cole dropped her off at her apartment, Jordan woke up Mrs. S and made sure she got back to her place, and then checked on her mom before heading into the bathroom for a shower.

It'd been a long day. An exciting day. A completely incredible day.

Cole had come back. And for a little while in that

hangar, she'd thought it might be possible to be completely head over heels, happy, sappy, in love.

Which only confirmed her long-held belief that she was an idiot. When would she get it through her thick skull? Brenner women never attracted the commitment type of guy.

He's leaving for Texas on Monday.

Wanting Cole felt like an obsession. And she'd watched enough addicts gamble away their life savings to know any kind of dependence was a bad thing. She wished he hadn't told her about the hospital. Why had she even asked? Why couldn't she have just enjoyed the meal and kept things light and fun? Or better yet, why couldn't she have had wild abandoned sex on that table in that hangar and let that be all there was to it? Did she need love and commitment to have great sex? No.

So, she'd have wild abandoned sex tomorrow night. Enjoy one last time with Cole before he left. All she had to do was remember they were two people who found each other mutually attractive, and that she'd made a rational decision to enjoy some damn fine sex.

As long as she refused to allow herself to feel anything more for him, she'd be okay.

Because she didn't want to open herself up to the pain of loving him.

Although, she was afraid it might be too late.

10

MITCH PUNCHED the mute button on his remote when he heard the apartment door open and slam closed. "Hey, how'd the dinner go?"

"Great." Jackson's keys landed with a clink in the mosaic bowl on the entry table. A moment later he flopped down on the other end of the sofa and propped his dress shoes on the coffee table. "Who's winning?"

"You're home kind of early for 'great.'" Mitch stabbed at his Chinese take-out with cheap wooden chopsticks.

"Well, we can't all be Casanovas like you— Oh wait. *You* aren't getting any, either."

"I got a week and a half left, Jackson. Then we'll see who's getting some." Twelve more rotten days.

Not that he minded Jackson bunking with him. He couldn't bring a woman back to his apartment right now anyway. And having Jackson around kept Mitch's mind off what he couldn't have.

Except tonight. Jackson had gone to that Keno girl's graduation.

"So, she wasn't impressed with your cooking, huh?"

"Turn the sound up, will ya?" Jackson got up and grabbed a beer from the fridge.

"You know, I would've left the apartment if you'd called."

Jackson chugged his beer and pinned him with a look. "You must be going postal without a woman for the past three weeks."

"Eighteen days. But who's counting?" Eighteen days without a woman's soft skin and plump breasts, and inane chatter. His life had been reduced to pool and TiVo. It was TiVo on a hi-def, fifty-two-inch, flat-screen TV. But still.

And what was worse, after that first agonizing week, he'd admitted that what he missed most was the distraction a woman gave him from the tedium of his existence. Every damn day, he wished his request for combat duty hadn't been denied.

It wasn't that he didn't like instructing. He spent his days teaching a couple of aerodynamics classes and taking his Raptor up to illustrate various combat maneuvers. At the end of the day what did he have to show for it?

"Eighteen days." Jackson whistled through his teeth. "Must be some sort of record for you." He shot Mitch a wicked grin. "Are women still showing up at your office?"

Mitch grunted, suppressing a grin. "I'll get Hughes back."

Her prank had actually been the most excitement he'd had in a long time. He'd forgotten how much he enjoyed razzing Hughes until she'd transferred here from D.C. And though he acted pissed about losing the bet, getting Hughes riled up had actually turned out to be kind of fun.

"So, are you seeing the Keno girl again?"

"What's with you and women's names?"

"It's rule number one. Always give them a nickname. That way they feel special and I don't call one by the wrong name in an unguarded moment."

Jackson shook his head. "You and your rules."

"Hey, don't knock what you haven't tried." Ever since his divorce, Mitch had established his "rules" for dating. Rules were crucial for making sure a woman knew up front what was on the menu.

"You're not seeing her tomorrow night, are you?"

"Not that it's any of your business, but yes."

"No, no, Jackson. That's a big mistake. Remember rule number three."

Rule number two was a given: no overnights. But rule number three was crucial also: no more than three dates. There was something about that fourth date that gave a woman the idea that he was serious about her. He'd learned that the hard way.

"I'm picking her up after her shift."

Mitch shook his head. Poor sap. But Jackson hadn't been out of the hospital all that long. Mitch could be magnanimous. "I'll see if I can vacate the premises tomorrow night."

"It's not that kind of— Oh, hell, McCabe you've got a one-track mind."

"And since when have you not? Don't tell me you might have—" he swallowed "—*feelings* for this girl."

Jackson gestured toward the TV. "Un-mute it. I want to catch the score."

"Jackson, I'm serious. That's a road that can only lead to FUBAR, man."

Jackson just stared at his beer can. "Not for everyone."

"But for guys like you and me, hell, yeah, it is."

Jackson shot off the sofa, his features contorted. "Well, maybe I'm not like you."

Mitch thunked his take-out carton on the coffee table and stood to face him. "Come on, man. You aren't the marrying kind. You ever get married, I'll go another month!"

"Hell, who said anything about marriage?"

"Oh, man." Mitch grabbed his chest. "You really had me going for a minute. Gave me a freakin' heart attack."

Jackson plopped back onto the sofa. "Would you really go another month without a woman if I married her?"

"I might have to swear off women all together if you did something so stupid."

Jackson mumbled into his folded arms, "Stupid is right."

GRABBING Cole's jacket from her locker, Jordan raced out of the dressing room at The Grand to the parking garage.

Cole was waiting beside his bike, wearing jeans and a dark brown button-down shirt. Her stomach flipped, her heart pounded, and she closed her eyes. She needed a moment to resist the urge to run into his arms, press her cheek to his chest, and squeeze him tightly. Why did the mere sight of him have to affect her this way? "I brought your jacket back." With one last longing glance, she held it out to him.

But he didn't take it.

When she looked into his eyes, blatant appreciation in his perusal warmed her from the inside out. "Keep it. I like picturing you wearing it."

Oh, no. Knowing she couldn't, Jordan took a deep breath then dropped her arm to her side.

"Hungry?"

"Starved."

"Well, hop on." He swung his leg over the bike and then helped her climb on. She secured her backpack over both shoulders and tucked his jacket in one of the saddle bags, intending to "forget" it there later.

As he pulled the bike into traffic, she hugged his waist and enjoyed the play of his chest muscles beneath her palms. The body-warmed cotton of his shirt held the musky scent that was all Cole. Oh, she could *so* get used to this. Yet that was not on the agenda.

All too soon he parked in the garage at the Venetian and they were strolling inside. He'd taken her hand to help her off the bike and hadn't let go, and the contact sent heat sizzling all over her body.

Then they stepped inside the lobby and Jordan's gaze was drawn up. Straight above her. The ceilings were painted in the style of the Old Masters. Sublime cherubs and angels seemed to look down and ridicule her meager attempts to remain unmoved tonight. Gleaming marble floors, elaborate sculptures and Grecian columns completed the awe-inspiring grandeur and elegance that was the Venetian Hotel. "Wow."

"You've never been here before?"

"Not in all my spare time. Can you imagine?" Sarcasm was her only defense.

He grinned as they turned a corner and he ushered her into the Grand Lux Café. The meal was beautifully prepared. Exquisite cuisine considering it was after two in the morning, but it might as well have been cheap burgers for all Jordan tasted of it.

After dinner, they made their way through the hotel to the front doors. The gondolas that glided down the Grand Canal sat empty and idle. Another mocking reminder that this romantic evening wasn't going anywhere. They had no future. Men like Cole, and his buddy McCabe, would never be tied down to one woman.

The strip never closed, but the pirates of Treasure Island across the boulevard had long since gone to bed, and the Dancing Waters of the Bellagio were still, the music silent. Jordan stood on the sidewalk, holding in a crushing sense of loss that threatened to overwhelm her.

Cole took her hand, rubbing his thumb over the back. "Come on." He tugged her north, away from the taunting tourist attractions.

But Jordan dug in her heels. "Even the Stratosphere Tower is closed this late."

He gazed down at her. "It doesn't matter. We can just walk." The way he looked at her, and the tone of his voice told her he meant it. That tonight, he just wanted to be with her.

And even though she'd promised herself she wouldn't, even though she'd given herself a stern talking-to earlier this evening, she fell.

It was just the stupidest thing she could've done. She'd fallen in love with another player. But it felt wonderful. Freeing. She wanted to throw her arms in the air and spin around, and shout it to the world. Her joy was back.

After Ian had left her stranded and penniless, happiness and fun had been replaced by bitterness and fear that she'd labeled common sense and prudence. She forgot that protecting oneself against pain also meant giving up the pleasures of being in love.

"Jordan?" He fingered a curl hanging down over her eye.

She'd never be sure if it was the light brush of his finger against her temple or the way he said her name that made her breath catch. But something passed between them. Something unspoken, and very real.

He lowered his head and kissed her gently, his mouth exploring hers with leisure. Jordan was in no mood for caution. Her hands locked around his waist and she poured all her passion and emotion into returning his kiss.

With a groan, he tore his mouth from hers and held her. "What am I going to do about you?"

Jordan blinked back stinging tears. "There's nothing for you *to* do. I'm living the life I want to live. And so are you."

"Maybe." He took her hand and led her up Las Vegas Boulevard.

Silence fell between them as they traveled past the ringing slots of casinos, the real world in Sin City. What did he mean by "maybe"? He certainly wasn't going to quit the Air Force and stay in Vegas with her. She wouldn't want him to. And she wasn't going to give up her independence for a man again.

At least she had the maturity to recognize the hope-lessness of this situation and the strength to keep her feelings to herself.

After a few blocks they came to the seedier part of the Strip; Cole's grip on her hand tightened and his eyes searched their surroundings for danger. Ever the warrior. His sharp-eyed gaze reminded her of a hawk—she froze in her tracks.

"Cole. I know something we can do." In that instant it seemed to her the entire evening had been leading up to this. "Come with me." She grinned and began jogging farther north, tugging him along with her.

"WHERE are you taking me, woman? You're not trying to hustle me, are you?" Cole teased as he loped along behind her. He returned her playful grin. The evening had seemed melancholic, but now the sparkle had returned to her eyes.

"You'll see," she answered. "Just another half a block." She stopped abruptly, gesturing to a storefront with a flourish of her arms. "Ta-da!"

Cole read the flashing neon sign. 24-Hour Tattoos.

"You want to get your new hawk done?" she asked.

His throat closed up. This was the perfect time. The perfect night. The perfect city. And the perfect person to be with to have it done. He grinned and nodded. "Why not?"

The tattoo artist was an older Asian man, with a long gray beard. He wore a ripped leather vest and had no visible patch of skin uninked. He said his name was Snake in a deep voice with an all-American accent.

While Cole selected a hawk, Jordan noted the walls covered with drawings to choose from.

"What about you?" He came up behind her. "Want to get one?"

She was staring at a drawing and biting her thumbnail. "I've always wanted one. But—"

"A spider?"

She shrugged. "I've loved spiders ever since I read *Charlotte's Web* in second grade. They're so dedicated. Working tirelessly all night to build a new web, making such a difference in so many lives, never giving up."

"Cool," he replied. "Get one…" He raised a finger. "Right…" Not quite touching her, his finger moved from the top of her breast over her shoulder and down to the small of her back.

Her gaze followed his finger until it disappeared behind her shoulder, and she stiffened when he touched the indention just above her heart-shaped buttocks. "There."

"Oh." Seemingly enticed by the idea, she stared at him. Her mouth was only an inch away. Her lips parted and he would have kissed her, but she pulled back and shook her head. "No."

"No kiss?"

"No, I don't think I'll get the tattoo tonight."

"Why not?" He grinned and nudged her elbow with his. "Too wild for you?"

She scrunched up her nose and stuck her tongue out at him. "Only to my budget."

The sight of that little pink tongue darting out between her lips sent his pulse racing. "Stick that thing out again." He lowered his head, filing away the information about her budget, but intent on kissing her.

She raised her chin and closed her eyes. Mmm, those lips.

"You ready?" Snake's gruff voice interrupted Cole's plan.

"Yes, sir." He strode over to the chair and took off his shirt before sitting down, explaining to Snake where he wanted the tattoo placed on his left arm.

Snake examined what was left of the hawk on his right arm. "That an Air Force insignia? You want it the same on the left?"

"Yes, sir."

"You get that in Iraq?" Snake asked, gesturing to Cole's scarred torso.

"Yep."

Snake was quiet for a moment, then said, "No charge." He turned away to gather his instruments.

Cole started to object. He appreciated the sentiment, but he refused to let his scars make him a charity case. Then he had a thought. "Can I pay for mine and get the lady's for free?"

As if he'd expected the request, Snake nodded. "Sure."

He looked over at Jordan, who was watching him

with a mixture of excitement and nervousness. "I don't know…I shouldn't, but…" She shrugged. "I can't let you think I'm boring."

He nearly choked. "Jordan. One thing you are not," he said, his gaze roaming down her curvaceous body, "is boring. I think you'd always manage to surprise me no matter how long I knew you."

She pursed her lips and folded her arms. "Tonight is an aberration, believe me. Normally, I'm very level-headed. I don't usually let myself take foolish risks."

"Taking risks makes life exciting."

She crossed her arms and pursed her lips. "Says the adrenaline junkie. Life is all about foolish risks for you, but some people have responsibilities."

The words cut him like a shaving nick, although he knew what she said was true. "So—" he gave her a mock-serious look "—you made a level-headed decision to go with me that night out into the desert?"

Her gaze concentrated on him, her eyes narrowed and one brow strategically raised. "Okay, maybe not. But at least I didn't choose you from across a crowded casino on a bet."

"Ouch!" He grabbed his chest and pulled out the invisible blade. "Touché." He grinned down at her and she chuckled. "I love the sound of your laugh," he told her.

Her grin got smaller as she gazed at him, but a smile still played around her lips. "Thank you. That was a nice thing to say."

"I wasn't being nice." He stared into her amazing eyes, refusing to look away first.

Finally, she broke eye contact. "Can I squeeze your hand when it's my turn?"

He smiled. "As hard as you want."

As the tattooist worked on his arm, Cole sat stoically, afraid that the smallest wince might make Jordan change her mind. And he wanted her to have that spider on her tailbone. The thought of it, of knowing she was doing something wild, something just for her, really got to him. He couldn't take his eyes from hers. She sat and watched him with a small smile of encouragement. Once, she reached up to push long blond strands of her hair away from her face and he longed to touch her. To kiss her. But it was more than just a physical yearning. Something deeper was happening to him. Something he didn't even want to explore. If he did, it might change everything. And he'd had enough change in his life already.

When it was her turn, she didn't hesitate and he admired her even more because he could sense her fear. She had to climb onto a table, on her stomach, and slide her jeans down just a bit while Snake tucked thick paper towels around her waistband.

At her first grimace, she reached out and Cole took her hand. She needed him. And it felt…not bad to be needed. "So, tell me all about growing up in Iowa. Must've been cool to live in one place your whole life."

Resting her chin on her arm, she closed her eyes. "Cedar Falls is a whole other world away from Vegas. Slower-paced. Friendly people. In school, kids could be cruel sometimes—I, um, developed early—but I had a few good friends." She squeezed his hand hard as the needle buzzed, and he almost wished he hadn't encouraged her. He didn't like knowing she was in pain.

"It was just Mom and me, but she made sure we had permanence in our lives. There's security in that. I can't imagine moving around all the time."

He shrugged. "That's the life of an Air Force brat. Went to six schools in ten years. My mom was great about the moving, though. Her dad was Air Force, too, so she knew what she was getting into. She always made friends with other officers' wives and had her bowling nights out. Poor Dad, stuck with all five of us kids every week."

"You think he felt stuck? Was he…resentful?"

At on time, Cole would have said yes, but since his recent conversation with his father… Now, he searched his memory for those nights he and his brothers and sisters were left alone with his dad and all he could remember were fun times around the kitchen table learning to play poker. "No, now that you mention it. I guess that was just my take on it."

"Must have been how my dad felt," she said quietly. "He didn't want to get stuck with me. So he took off before I was born."

Cole brought his other hand up to smooth her hair down the back of her head. "I'm sorry."

"It's funny." Her brows drew together. "I don't think I realized until just now, but I don't really miss having a dad. You can't miss something you never had. Sure, I'd look at other girls, my friends, with their dads and wonder.

Mostly, I think I felt the absence for my mom. She tried not to show it, but I think she was lonely pretty often."

Lonely. Yeah. Cole pictured himself in San Antonio. Alone.

But wasn't that the way he liked it?

She opened her eyes and looked at him strangely. "It's funny how our lives never turn out the way we think they will when we're kids."

"Yeah, I always thought I'd be the first man on Mars. Now I'd settle for piloting a space shuttle."

"I bet you will someday." She smiled at him with lips tightened.

A familiar spasm rose up from his chest to form a lump in his throat. He swallowed past it, forced it back down to the deepest part of his soul. Space was a dream he had to let go of.

"How does it look?" she asked, interrupting his thought.

Cole leaned over to look, focusing more on the soft skin of her back and delicate line of her spine than the sore and bloody spot at her tailbone. "Great." His hand was completely numb from her squeezing it so tightly, but he didn't mind.

After Snake announced he was done, she hopped down and tried to look in a mirror, but it was still so swollen and red, the spider was barely recognizable.

She grinned even as her eyes sparkled with tears, and whatever had shifted inside him when he first learned about her mother moved another notch.

"Thank you." She thrust out her right hand to Snake

and shook hands with him, then, after Cole paid and they were on the sidewalk again, she threw her arms around his waist and hugged him. "Thank you, too."

"You're welcome." His voice had turned hoarse. He held her tightly against him and kissed the pulse at her temple, aching to be with her, in her. But first he would tell her everything. He cleared his throat. "You asked me last night if I was anxious to return to Iraq."

She pulled back to look at him. "Yes?"

"I won't be returning to combat. I want to. But I can't. I can't fly anymore." Now that he'd said the words out loud, it felt as if a noose had been loosened from his neck.

Her eyes widened. "Why not?"

"The explosion burst my right eardrum. I'm deaf in that ear, and my equilibrium is shit." He stopped in his tracks, the core of his fear spilling out. "And if I'm not a fighter pilot, what the hell am I?"

She reached out to him, and her delicate hand touching his arm steadied him. "I don't know what you'll end up doing, but there's more to you than being a fighter pilot. I believe when bad things happen to us, we can choose to see it as an opportunity to make something good come from it. If you search hard enough, you'll find what you were meant to do."

Her words slammed into him, burning their way deep into his soul. He tugged her into his arms and swept his mouth over hers. Letting go of despair. Giving her, without words, a part of that soul. When he held Jordan, his life didn't seem so empty. Hope was a living thing.

He wanted this night with her. Wanted to wake in the morning in her arms. He trailed hot kisses along her jaw. "Jordan, don't go home," he begged in her ear. He needed her. He needed her soft body in his arms, her luscious flesh filling his hands. "Stay with me tonight." Unsure, he stepped away to gauge her reaction.

Her eyes were dark with passion and her lips curved in a half smile. "I already asked Mrs. S to spend the night with my mom," she whispered.

11
_____

ALEX WAS in a nasty mood as she answered her apartment doorbell. Whoever the hell was bothering her at this time of night better be warning her of flood or fire.

She swung open the door growling, and then blinked in shock. "Mitch?" Oh, damn. She never called him by his first name. What was he doing here?

"Hey, Hughes." Mitch shoved past her and dropped his duffel beside her couch. "Jackson texted me a while ago. He's having company over, said to make myself scarce."

"At four o'clock in the morning? Why didn't he just get a room?"

"Uh, I don't know." He headed for her kitchen, yanked open the fridge and started rummaging around. "Maybe cause she works at a hotel. You got any pickles?" He pulled out lunch meat and bread and sliced cheese and set the items on the counter.

"It's Jordan?" She stood behind him in the kitchen.

"Yeah, that Keno girl. You want a sandwich?"

Alex couldn't believe it. She knew Jackson had come back to town, but she'd thought the woman was too smart to see him again.

He grabbed a plate from her cabinet and started building a Dagwood sandwich. "Yeah, I guess that's her name. So, anyway. I can't be around women right now, therefore, I figured I'd crash here tonight."

Alex ground her teeth. Hot fury rose up from her core and her body shook. That was twice now he'd insinuated she wasn't a woman. What was she, some sort of genderless humanoid life form?

She pictured herself shoving him to the tile floor, ripping off her shorts and tank top and showing him just how genderless she was *not*. Once she had him at her mercy, she'd unbuckle his belt, yank off his T-shirt and jeans and kiss him senseless. Push her fingers through his sandy-blond hair, run her palms over his hard chest—oh, jeez. Had she really just been thinking of her best bud in that way?

Her chest rose and fell in uneven breaths; she'd soaked her panties. She snapped to attention, finding Mitch munching away on her food, oblivious.

"Hey, tomorrow's Sunday. You want to head out to Hoover and catch some white water?" He leaned a hip against her counter and wiped his mouth on her one and only kitchen towel.

Alex growled. How could she have a lustful fantasy about this Neanderthal? "I have plans."

He stopped chewing. "What plans?"

She snorted. "Do you think I sit around waiting to see if you want to go do something?"

His face scrunched up in confusion. "What's your problem lately?"

"I am not at your beck and call, McCabe. My life does not revolve around you." Alex folded her arms.

"O-okay." He swallowed and looked down at his sandwich. "Are you sure you don't have any pickles?"

Arrgh! Now Alex's fantasy involved her hands around his neck, crushing the air out of him until he apologized. She shook it off and drew in a cleansing breath. The clueless jerk wasn't worth the effort. "Just clean up your mess when you're done." She forced herself to turn and head back for her bedroom. Like she'd get any more sleep tonight with him out there on her couch.

Because Captain Mitchell McCabe always slept butt-naked.

JORDAN HESITATED at the entry to McCabe's apartment as Cole unlocked the door and led her inside. The place was so obviously set for seduction. The home of a player.

There was a bottle of wine chilling in an ice bucket next to two wineglasses on the bar, and mood lighting had been left on, along with some soft music. She should feel weird that this was McCabe's bachelor lair, or insulted that Cole had been so sure of her.

But she wasn't.

She wanted this night. This last time with him. She'd had the cab ride back to The Grand and the long motorcycle ride to this apartment complex to think about everything.

Cole had given her a gift he didn't even realize. Being with him she'd learned to let go of fear and embrace the joy life can sometimes bring. And most importantly, she'd forgiven herself for a youthful impulsive decision.

"I'm going to kill McCabe," Cole growled as he grabbed a remote off the entry table, turned off the music and turned up the lights. "I didn't tell him to do this." He looked back at her, his expression hardened.

"Don't worry about it." She moved close and slid her arms around his neck. "Just kiss me." She rose on her toes and brought her mouth to his. For a split second she felt him freeze beneath her, but then he swept her into his arms and moved his lips over hers, barely restrained. He fumbled to untie the back of her blouse, but she caught his hand. "I want to undress you first this time."

His eyes flared but he dropped his hands to his sides and waited.

Slowly, she unbuttoned his shirt, placing kisses at each new area of skin revealed. Once his shirt hung open, she trailed her lips down his abdomen and his stomach twitched. When she glanced up, she noticed the little muscle in his jaw tense. Her hands moved down to unbuckle his belt and she followed her finger's path with her lips.

She'd come this far in the role of aggressor, might as well go all the way. Slowly, she unzipped his jeans, then slid her hands under his briefs, and pushed both down. His erection popped free, jutting from a nest of black curls. His hands clenched at his sides.

Her job required her to tolerate a certain amount of objectification, but now the tables were turned. She was still fully dressed while he was exposed. A feeling of power surged inside her.

He'd pursued her so aggressively, she didn't think he was normally the kind of guy to let a woman take the lead. Yet he waited patiently as she decided on her next move.

Just one finger at first, gliding over the slick head, then her palm cupped his balls and her other hand gripped the hot, pulsing shaft.

With a tortured growl, he grabbed her wrist. "I won't last if you do that," he warned.

But she wasn't in a cautious mood. "Let's see how long you can take it." She held his gaze as she sank to her knees and licked just the swollen tip, tasting him. Wanting more, she took him fully in her mouth and swirled her tongue around as she sucked and slid him back out and in again.

He groaned and cursed.

She glanced up. His eyes were closed, his head thrown back. His chest rose and fell and his stomach muscles jerked as her tongue worked along the shaft, teasing him. When she took him deep again, he gripped her head and let out a muffled grunt.

His fingers tangled in her hair, lifting her face to take her mouth in a powerful, bruising kiss. Then he straightened and stared at her. "Where did you come from?"

"Iowa," she answered blithely.

He grabbed her under the arms, lifted her to her feet, and covered her mouth with his. His kiss was rough, demanding, as he plunged his tongue deep inside. Then he pulled back and stared at her, a question in his eyes. But all he said was "Jordan." His fingers played with the soft shell of her ear as he kissed her gently this time, nipping at her lips.

Over and over he uttered her name like a prayer as he kissed down the line of her jaw and into the hollow of her neck. Sweeping her blouse off her shoulder, his hand slipped beneath her bodice to cup her breast over her lacy bra and rub his thumb over the nipple.

She gripped his thick black hair as he reached around, untied her top, and pulled it over her head along with her bra. With exquisite tenderness, he cupped her breasts in his palms and squeezed. It was her turn to moan as he took a nipple in his mouth and suckled.

"So sweet," he mumbled. He drew her nipple in, tickled it with his tongue and then moved to the other one.

She rocked her pelvis forward at the sudden sharp ache at her core.

As he unbuttoned and unzipped her jeans, she encircled his erection and pumped him with a slow steady pull. With a guttural moan he yanked her jeans down her legs, and off, then clutched her bottom and lifted her against him. With long strides he carried her down a hall into a bedroom, laid her on the bed and followed her down.

While he produced a shiny packet from his wallet, tore it open and rolled on protection, she pulled off her panties. Their gazes locked as he clasped her under the knees, fitted himself to her and pushed in with a low groan.

The bed shook as he began a rhythmic thrust, pushing forcefully into her, and Jordan locked her ankles around his waist. He angled his hips to stroke her G-spot while one hand slid between them to find her clit. She moaned and squirmed her hips beneath his steady, determined technique. He played her body with delicate precision, exactly what she'd expect of a man accustomed to performing dangerous maneuvers at supersonic speeds.

Colored lights exploded behind her closed eyes, and she cried out as powerful contractions spiraled up and consumed her. "Cole!"

Overwhelmed. Amazed at the surge of emotion each time they came together. She clung to him as her body wound down from a sensual explosion of heart-squeezing pleasure.

All her muscles trembling, Jordan held him as he made that sound that was half gasp, half grunt and rocked against her one last time. Her love for him expanded as she lay in his arms, at the sound of his moan, and the way he said her name when he came.

His breathing was so harsh she felt each warm puff of air on her neck as he nuzzled beneath her ear. One of his hands still clutched her butt. The other one played with her hair, making her shiver. "I couldn't stop thinking about you in Phoenix. I had to see you again."

Jordan gripped his shoulders and squeezed her eyes shut. He was still hard inside her. They were still one. "How long will you be in San Antonio?"

"I don't know. A couple of years, maybe. If these job interviews don't pan out, would you consider job-hunting in Texas?"

She stilled. Was he asking what she thought he was?

Mr. I-could-never-see-myself-with-a-mortgage? "I…I'd have to think about it."

"Fair enough." Before he withdrew, he took her mouth once more, kissing her with a desperate heat that she returned. Then he slid off the bed and padded to the bathroom.

Jordan rolled to her side and hugged a wayward pillow, watching him as he came back and climbed in beside her, folding her in his arms.

"Cole. I know we only have now. And that's okay."

SINKING DOWN, skin to skin with Jordan, Cole tightened his hold. She was his oasis in the midst of a barren desert. And he wasn't ready to let her go. "I'm not sure it's okay with me. This can't be the last time I ever see you."

"Well, maybe you can visit me sometime." He had a leg thrown over one of hers and her free foot rubbed his calf as she stared into his eyes.

He shook his head and cupped her face. "I think I want more."

"Already?" The smile she gave him didn't reach her eyes.

Cole frowned. How could she even try to joke about this? "I'm serious, Jordan."

Her false smile faded. "I know. But I don't think there's any solution right now. Let's enjoy every moment tonight. Kiss me, Cole."

He wasn't ready to drop the subject. Perhaps he'd have better luck discussing it if he pleasured her senseless.

Ducking his head, he began pressing open-mouthed

kisses down her body. His hands caressed where his lips touched. The firm plumpness of her breasts, the little mole beneath her right nipple. The dimple of her belly button, the solid plane of her pelvic bone. She was firm yet curvy in all the right places. Her skin was like the finest silk.

Running his fingers through the dark blond curls at the apex of her thighs, he pushed her legs wide and bent his head to drink from her nourishing nectar. "I want you like this every night," he mumbled as he suckled deeper. "Wouldn't you like that, too?"

She dug her nails into his scalp and moaned. "Yes."

"Then come with me to Texas." He pushed a finger inside her.

"Cole. Don't." She writhed beneath him.

"I need you there." He added a finger and suckled harder, teasing her with his tongue.

Her only response was unintelligible syllables and he gave up for the moment, concentrating instead on bringing her to orgasm. And once that mission was accomplished, he began all over again until finally he had to be inside her.

Entwining his fingers with hers above her head, he thrust his hips and sank deep, deeper, until he felt a part of her. As he clung to her hands, pulled out and thrust back in, his mind burst into sensory overload, out of control. He felt himself come apart deep inside.

It was like hitting four Gs, taking his Raptor into a roll, and feeling the pop of breaking the sound barrier all at once, and Cole could only hold on and ride it out.

His brain turned to mush and his body liquefied beside hers as his world was reduced to a blur of damp flesh and the feel of soothing fingers in his hair. And he knew wherever she was, was home.

A MUFFLED sound woke Jordan.

Mom?

She tried to roll off the couch but strong arms tightened around her, and a large hand covered her breast.

The sleepy haze fell away and the incredibly soft high-thread-count sheets told her she wasn't on the couch in her apartment, but in Cole's—McCabe's—apartment.

She was nestled against Cole, his chest to her back, his groin soft beneath her bottom. Damp with sweat, his body was like a furnace engulfing her. Even her perpetually freezing toes were warm and toasty. She wiggled them and felt the hair on his legs, so crisp and masculine. Lying there, she soaked up the comfort of being held by a strong man while she slept, waking up beside someone and feeling…not so alone.

Except for a small split between the panels, the heavy bedroom curtains kept out even the bright lights of Vegas and she could barely see her hand before her face. With the clock on his side of the bed, she had no clue what time it was. After they'd made love a second time, he'd slipped into a profoundly deep sleep.

But, no wonder, after the way his whole body had strained and trembled. His need had been a living thing. His expression had been unreadable, but his eyes had held a storm of emotions. Confusion. Resentment. Profound sadness.

His powerful emotions had transferred to her and resulted in more than just a physical climax. She'd wanted to weep uncontrollably. The rush of oneness she'd felt in his arms only made it harder to refuse his invitation to Texas. She couldn't and wouldn't run off with a man again when she had no job and no money. And then there was her mom.

His body jerked and he cried out, then reared away and rolled to his back, awake now. She could hear it in his rapid breathing, feel it in his tenseness.

She turned to face him and put a hand on his chest. "You okay?"

"Yeah." He cleared his throat. "I'm good." She heard him rubbing the rough stubble on his jaw.

She wished she could see his face. Intent on turning on a lamp, she scooted away. But he gripped her hip and rolled on top of her. "Where you going?" His voice was gruff.

"Cole." She brushed the hair off his forehead and wriggled beneath him. "I'm only turning on a light."

His body relaxed and he eased off her. "Could you not?"

"Okay." She waited. When she'd first met Cole, he'd been confident verging on cocky, on the prowl and unapologetic for it. Did he regret letting her see him so vulnerable now?

"It's the same nightmare," he said quietly. His hand found hers and clasped it. "I have it almost every night." She felt rather than saw him shrug. "Doc says it's normal."

Jordan turned to face him, brought their entwined hands up to her lips and kissed his knuckles. "Is your dream about being shot down?"

"After. It took me a couple of days to get back to forward base, traveling through hostile environment."

"Oh, Cole! After you'd been burned so badly?"

His grip tightened. "In my dream, I can't find the base. And I know I'm never going to make it back. But I did. So, why do I keep having these damn nightmares?"

She scooted closer to lay her head on his chest and he circled his arms around her. His heart beat strong and fast beneath her ear. She ran her hand down his arm, and up to smooth his brow. "Maybe you're still searching for home."

He stilled and his breathing stopped.

Did she really just say that? Once the words were out, she realized how they sounded. Would he think she was agreeing that she should make her home with him? Even if she were willing to actually trust a man not to abandon her, she couldn't move her mom away from everything familiar. "I mean, maybe once you're settled in to your new assignment, you'll stop having them."

His chest rose as he drew in a deep breath. "Maybe." He rolled until she was beneath him and lowered his head for a tender kiss. "You're probably as sick of hearing me talk as I am." He gave her another soft kiss as he smoothed her tangled hair out over the pillow. "Thanks for listening." A deeper kiss this time, his lips stirring sensually over hers. He moved his hips and she felt his hard length press against her thigh.

As weak sunlight peeped in from the opening in the curtains, he made slow, sweet love to her. In contrast to the turbulent coupling earlier, he refused to be hurried now. Every touch was deliberate, every kiss lingering. By the time Jordan fell into an exhausted sleep, dawn had come and gone.

The next time she awoke, it was to the sound of a cell phone ringing somewhere far away. Not even sure she'd heard it, she sluggishly sat up, shoving hair out of her face. The clock showed eight-thirty.

Cole lay on his stomach, his arms and legs sprawled across the mattress. The ring tone sounded again and this time she knew it was coming from her backpack. At the third ring, she climbed over him and ran for it, thinking to at least check caller ID.

The caller was her home number.

Mrs. Simco. Oh, no. She tried to slide it open to answer, but the ringing stopped and it went to voice mail. Her hands shaking, she steadied her breathing to call her back.

Mrs. Simco answered after the third ring.

"Mrs. S? Everything okay?"

"Jordan, honey." Alice Simco's voice quivered. "I wasn't sure what to do. I just woke up and your mama is gone."

12

JORDAN had to get home. Terror and guilt engulfed her. She never should have left her mom all night. "Call 911, and I'll be there in fifteen minutes."

As Jordan spoke, she was gathering up her clothes from the living-room floor. Then she remembered her panties were in the bedroom.

Cole stirred and rolled to face her as she dropped her phone and backpack on the bed. "What's going on?"

A thousand horrible images flashed in her mind as she pulled her clothes on. How long had Mom been gone? How far could she have traveled? Was she safe? Was she scared? *Oh please God, let me find her.*

Cole sat up and scrubbed his hands over his face. "Jordan?"

All Jordan could do was shake her head as she pulled on her jeans. If she tried to speak, the panic might escape past the snarling knot in her throat.

"Your mom?" Cole asked as he stood and grabbed his briefs and jeans.

Tears threatening, she nodded. "She's missing."

By the time she was dressed, so was Cole. For the

first time since she'd hung up the phone, she looked directly at him. Reasonable or not, guilt writhed in her like poisonous snakes. "I knew I shouldn't have left my mom for so long. If I hadn't been so damned selfish." She clamped her lips shut, darted to the front door and rushed out into the courtyard.

Before she was halfway to the parking lot, Cole had caught up with her. "I'm coming with you." His long stride had no trouble keeping up with her running.

"If you'll just give me a ride home."

"Of course. You think I'd make you take a cab?"

She bit back a horrible remark. He didn't deserve her anger.

"Jordan." Cole put his arm around her shoulders. "We'll find her. I'll call some of the guys from Nellis and we'll get a search party going."

Prickly tears threatened again. Crap. She couldn't fall apart now. She swallowed her emotions and strode to his motorcycle.

By the time they reached her apartment, a steely calm had settled over her. Her mother wore a Safe Return ID bracelet with the emergency 800 number to call if she was found. Surely someone would spot her now that daylight had broken. And the Las Vegas police understood about Alzheimer's patients. While Jordan answered the detective's questions and found a recent picture, Cole pulled out his cell phone and made a few calls.

Within half an hour search and rescue teams had been formed to comb the area. A canine unit and even a police helicopter were dispatched, and dozens of off-duty military personnel began showing up, offering to make flyers and distribute them.

"Let's go." Cole held out his hand. "We'll take my bike and you can direct me to the places you think your mom might go."

Leaving a willing Mrs. Simco to coordinate search efforts at the apartment, Jordan climbed on behind Cole. No way could she wait around the apartment doing nothing.

Cole drove her to the familiar areas first: the coin laundry, the grocery store, the college campus. Then they expanded their search to what seemed like every neighborhood on the west side of town, even taking back roads and alleys, crossing vacant fields and driving along park trails where a car could never have gone.

As the morning turned to afternoon, and the afternoon to evening with no sign of her mom, Jordan's panic ratcheted up to sheer terror. Every time she began to fall apart, to lose hope, Cole was right there beside her, encouraging her, assuring her that they would find her mother, never giving up and, more importantly, never letting her give up.

But dusk was settling in, the sun dropping behind the mountains and they still hadn't found her. Jordan had hoped the evening news programs running her picture might generate at least a tip, but her cell phone remained silent as Cole pulled out of a suburban neighborhood on the very edge of the city limits and headed back to her apartment.

Mrs. Simco was playing solitaire at the kitchen table with the cordless phone beside her spread-out cards. She stood and offered to make them sandwiches.

The thought of eating made Jordan nauseous. She declined, but Cole frowned and moved to the table, touching the cards.

Snapping his fingers, he swiveled to face her. "Have you taken your mom to a football game since she moved to Vegas?" He sounded excited. "Or would she have at least seen a stadium?"

Adjusting her train of thought from despair to this out-of-the-blue question, Jordan blinked. "We're not exactly football fans. I don't think—wait, there's the stadium at UNLV. Mom would've seen it on the way to the campus with me a couple of times. Why?"

"The cards reminded me. Something your mom said when we were playing Gin. She called me Jeff and kept talking about meeting under the bleachers after the football game. It's a long shot, but…"

A chill hissed up her spine. "Jeff is my father's name." She thumped his shoulder. "Let's go."

It took almost an hour to get the police to call campus security and explain. It was fully dark by the time the stadium gates were unlocked and the lights flickered on. With everything locked up, she didn't see how her mom had somehow slipped unseen inside locked gates, but perhaps it had been open earlier today. It didn't matter. Jordan wasn't leaving without looking.

The colossal stadium seemed a daunting task, so they split up. Cole took the west-facing bleachers and the security guard accompanied Jordan searching the east. With the guard by her side, she hiked half the length of the U-shaped stadium, checking every concession stand, bathroom and section of seats. Every dark corner she turned, hope would surge, only to be disappointed. Her mom wasn't here.

As she rounded the curved section she expected to meet Cole at the halfway point, but he wasn't anywhere in sight. They continued around, still checking every opening. At an entrance to the field, she saw him. He stood looking down at a large trash can in an alcove, his hair moving in the cool breeze.

Hope was tempered by dread. Had he found her? Was she all right? Jordan and the security guard raced up the concrete incline, but stopped short when Cole waved them back.

Huddled behind the plastic trash container sat her mom, looking haggard and petrified, but alive. Jordan clamped her hands over her mouth and broke down. Silent sobs wracked her as she tried to hold in the tears.

She heard Cole call her mother's name softly.

Tammy scrutinized him and then her face lit up. "Jeff! You're here!" She tried to stand but fell back and Cole dropped into a crouch and caught her.

"I'm so glad you came, Jeff." Her mom's voice croaked. "I have something important to tell you." Then the sparkle in her eyes died away and her expression crumpled in anguish. "You didn't come," she cried. "Why didn't you come? It's your baby, Jeff."

Jordan went cold inside and her heart broke. Oh,

Mom. She knew Mom had been abandoned. But to actually see and hear her pain.

Cole put a hesitant arm around her mom's shoulders. "I'm here now, Tammy. Come with me." When she didn't fight him, he scooped her up and she flung her arms around his neck and clung to him.

Seeing Cole's compassion, watching him carry her mother out of the stadium, Jordan lost all pretense that she didn't deeply love this man. The feeling was unlike anything she'd ever experienced. It wasn't blind infatuation or lust. No. This was the kind of love that lasts for life.

FOR COLE, the rest of the night became a blur of police conversations and ambulance sirens, and an unwanted news crew pestering him for the story and hailing him as a hero.

Used to be, after a long day of combat, he'd have handled the surge of adrenaline with a run around the base or a couple of hours lifting weights.

But tonight, dealing with all the drama left him drained, as though he'd slit open a vein and poured out everything he had to give. He wanted nothing more than to fall into a bed in a dark, quiet room and sleep for twenty-four hours. He wanted to disconnect.

Tammy was dehydrated but otherwise unharmed, and the hospital sent her home sedated and stable. Jordan had held up well through everything, remaining calm and in charge until her mother was tucked into bed and everyone had left. Once the last cop was out the door—throwing a parting joke to Cole about joining the force—and Mrs. S went home, Jordan seemed to sag before his eyes. She looked at him a moment and then her face crumpled.

Cole caught her in his arms and held her up. With a sob, she burrowed her nose into his chest. Her shoulders shook and he felt her tears wet his shirt.

"Shh, it's okay." He rubbed her back, murmuring soothing noises.

The breath left her body in a whimper and she molded herself against him, holding him. Her cry gurgled against his chest where she pressed her face. "What if you hadn't been here? I'd have never looked for her there."

"All that matters is we found her."

"But what if this happens again?" She snuggled into his arms and hugged tightly.

"Then we'll deal with it. I promise."

"No." She shook her head and stepped back. "Don't do that. Don't make promises you can't keep. You're all about living wild and reckless and I can't be that way. I have responsibilities."

Wait a minute. Why was he the bad guy here? He'd asked her to come to Texas, hadn't he? But—as dumb as it was—he hadn't thought about the repercussions moving would have on her mother. What if she took off again? Only this time in San Antonio where neither of them knew the area? Dealing with her mom would encompass a lot more than just an occasional card game and some cold cuts.

He understood now why she'd refused to discuss moving.

How had he gotten so involved in this woman's life? He couldn't have someone depending on him. Commitment had never been in his plan. How could he even think about any kind of future with someone? Especially when there were greater complications attached.

He stared into her big blue eyes, filled with grief and fear. And need. As their gazes locked, he wasn't sure how to explain. He cleared his throat.

Jordan's brows drew together and she jerked back, away from his reach. Her expression hardened. "You understand now, don't you?"

"It's not what you think. It's just—" He ran a shaky hand through his hair, trying to choke in a breath. Maybe he wanted to give it a try.

"It's just that you didn't think about my mom before, right?" Her voice was shaky.

"No, I didn't. But that doesn't mean we couldn't— But my life, right now. I don't know—"

"So, go. You have to be in Texas tomorrow morning." She waved a trembling hand toward the door.

Cole hesitated. He had to make her understand.

"Get out of here, Cole. You know that's what's best for both of us."

His brain was on overload. He didn't know what the hell he wanted. He had to take a step back, consider all this when he could think more clearly. Tightening his jaw, he spun on his heel and strode from her apartment.

JORDAN STOOD in frozen shock until well after the roar of Cole's Harley faded down the street.

She'd known this was coming. Known it would hurt like hell. She'd finally let herself love again. Need again. And the resulting pain was inevitable.

But what hurt the most was something she hadn't counted on. For the first time in her life, she'd experienced what it was like to have a man around to share the burden, to lean on. And now, having known such a feeling, she would miss it.

Her world shattered into choppy flashbacks of Cole reassuring her, of knowing he held her safe in his arms while she fell apart.

How could she do this on her own from now on? Her mother was only going to get worse. She grabbed her stomach and doubled over, dropped to her knees and sank to sit on her feet.

She wasn't sure how long she sat there, but she'd survived before. She would this time. It was her and Mom against the world. She'd pick up the pieces of her life once more and be okay. Again. By herself.

13

COLE ONLY stopped by McCabe's to get his duffel and gear. He was scheduled to report to his new commander at Lackland tomorrow at 0800 hours, but he'd missed his flight. Before catching the red-eye, he had a couple of free hours. And if there were no delays, he'd have just enough time to shower and shave in the officers' club at Lackland before reporting for duty.

For now he needed speed. And distance.

The desert night swallowed him up as he pushed his Harley to its limits. The sand spitting into his face and the lonely road curling out before him gave permission to his rage.

He'd wanted to comfort Jordan. What was so bad about that? And then, he'd only tried to be honest. But she hadn't wanted to listen. How was he supposed to think straight after such a grueling day? Her tears had torn him up. Hell, they still did.

Mile after mile, the roar of his bike's engine rumbled in his chest, feeding the restlessness. The arid desert, the spiny cacti, and along the horizon, the inflexible mountains all seemed to match his mood.

His throat felt dry as he pulled up next to a dilapidated adobe shack. It had to be one of the piss-poorest hole-in-the-wall joints north of the border. The place was full of bikers, served cheap tequila and no beer nuts.

The bartender was a Native American named Lucky Bear. Cole glanced around casually as he downed a shot. One of the bikers at the table behind him decided to look at him the wrong way. Cole knew that look. The guy seemed to have a problem with his military crew cut. Good. He was itching to plant his fist into someone's nose.

"What are you looking at?" he snarled, meeting the man's gaze, eager to take the first swing.

With a long-suffering sigh, the biker clenched his meaty hands on the table, shoved his chair back and slowly stood. He looked to be Grady's height: about six foot five, but this guy was massive, maybe three hundred pounds.

Adrenaline shot through Cole's veins. His knuckles clenched as he stood and got in the guy's face. Come on. Fight me, you long-haired freak.

Cole braced himself for impact, but the guy only smiled. "That Harley you rode in on. It got the staggered exhaust with the shorty dual mufflers?"

Cole blinked. "Uh, yeah."

The biker nodded. "I been thinking about getting myself a new bike. That's the XL 1200 C Sportster, huh?"

Just my luck I walk into the only bar in a thousand-mile radius with pacifist bikers. Cole gestured with his chin. "Yeah. Got a clutch so smooth you can make love and shift at the same time."

Next thing he knew, the bikers were buying him a shot of tequila for serving their country and Lucky Bear was asking him if he had woman trouble. At that, Cole decided it was time to head back to catch his flight. He'd come in here to take his mind *off* Jordan.

Still, as he sped away, her words kept creeping into his consciousness.

What had she called him? Wild and reckless? Irresponsible? And he was. Case in point: how he'd acted in that bar. He could have been seriously hurt. And that was why he'd never be good at relationships. Even if he decided he wanted the responsibilities that came with being with Jordan, it was too late. He'd screwed up. It was over for sure. And that was probably for the best.

The road came to a sharp curve and, instead of slowing down, Cole gunned it. Yeah. He *was* reckless, wasn't he? Acting responsibly was for other guys. He had nothing to tie him down. Nothing to lose.

He had nothing, period.

A jackrabbit darted in front of his bike and Cole slammed on the brakes and yanked the front wheel sideways. The bike skidded off the road, hit something and flipped.

COLE AWOKE with a gasp of much-needed air. Someone had detonated a bomb inside his head. In his mouth was the dusty, sour taste he'd come to associate with the desert. His body screeched in pain as if it'd been set afire. And something wet dripped from his hair and into his left eye.

What the hell?

Then he remembered. He'd been shot down some-where north of Baghdad. He'd ejected, but the explo-sion had sent burning shrapnel into his flight suit.

The sun's rays blazed white-hot. Cole judged it to be around midday. How long had he been out?

The Iraqis were quiet for now, but a rescue in hostile territory was tricky. He'd better get moving. Make his way to some cover before their midday prayers ended.

He tensed himself for worse pain and rolled to his hands and knees, then sat up holding an arm across his ribs. By concentrating on breathing, he managed the worst of the pain and used his sleeve to wipe blood from his eyes. Correction: what was left of his sleeve.

Blinking to clear his vision, he searched his sur-roundings. What was that off in the distance? Gritting his teeth, he pushed to his feet and squinted his eyes.

A U.S. highway sign?

The desert spun around him and images of his life since he'd been shot down flashed through his mind.

He wasn't in Iraq. He'd crashed his bike, not an F-22. Scanning the terrain, he saw its mangled metal glinting in the sun about thirty yards away. But that didn't mean he had to walk the rest of the way. Smiling, he reached in his jeans pocket for his cell phone. It came out in bits and pieces.

Son of a bitch.

"I COULD NEVER do this all the time." Alex—aka Captain Hughes—shifted from one combat boot to the other as Jordan sorted through racks of clothes.

"Who says I do this all the time?" When the going got tough, the tough went shopping, right? Today, Jordan was here out of sheer necessity, but it was still fun.

Her new friend didn't look so thrilled to be here. Alex's eyes looked glazed and her shoulders were hunched. Though it'd been Captain Hughes's—Alex's—choice to be here. She'd called Jordan this morning to check on how her mom was doing and asked if Jordan could meet for lunch.

Jordan needed to have a suit to interview in, and hadn't wanted to leave her mom for any longer than necessary, so they'd turned it into a shopping date instead. Jordan was determined to carry on. If nothing else, Mom getting lost yesterday and Cole leaving last night had only made getting a better job even more essential.

"I can't believe women go through all this just to attract a man."

"Hey, I'm getting this suit for a job interview I have tomorrow," Jordan clarified. "How about this one?" She held a conservatively cut navy suit jacket with a matching pencil skirt, both still on the hangers, against her body.

Alex shrugged. "I can't tell any difference from that last one."

"How can you say that? The other suit was black, and had an A-line skirt." Jordan was beginning to suspect Alex needed a crash course in Fashion 101.

"Honestly, Jordan, they look the same to me."

"Okay, let me try this on and then I'll be done. I have to be at the casino in an hour." Jordan took the suit into the dressing room, mentally calculating the Memorial

Day sale price, plus tax. Her savings for investing in job interviews were almost nil, however, this outlet price might mean she'd have enough to get the Calvin Klein pumps, as well.

She'd politely passed on asking Alex for her opinion on the shoes. What the girl needed was Beauty Boot Camp, Jordan decided. She could just picture Alex's petite yet athletic frame softened by the right style and fit of clothes. And some highlights in her brown hair would enhance her flawless complexion. Wouldn't it be fun to see if Cole even recognized her?

Cole. She had to quit dwelling on him. It was over.

Jordan took a deep breath and studied her reflection. The suit fitted her to perfection, even with her aggravatingly big chest. She stepped out of the dressing room and did her best runway pose and turn. "Well?"

"It's great. Let's go."

Jordan grimaced. "It'd have to be dry-cleaned. It's forty-four percent wool. But it's such a great price—"

"Jordan," Alex cut in. "You put less thought into screwing Jackson. Just buy it!"

Pain pierced her chest. It wasn't true. Was it?

"I'm sorry." Alex moaned. "I can't believe I said that. I can be such a bitch."

"No, you're right. There's definitely something wrong with me when it comes to choosing men. Charmers or daredevils, even quiet bankers, if they're allergic to commitment, I pick 'em." Or maybe it was just *her* they were allergic to.

"Hey. I have no room to judge. My best buddy is a

guy whose idea of commitment is buying the woman a drink before he nails her."

Jordan burst into an aborted sob. "How can you be friends with a man like that?" What was wrong with her? It took mentioning Cole's friend to make her lose it? She snatched her purse off the chair, scrambling for a tissue. She refused to get one teardrop on this fabulous suit.

Alex shrugged. "McCabe has his reasons for treating women the way he does, the sorry SOB."

"But how can you put up with it?"

Alex's face fell and she studied the steel toe of her combat boot. "I'm not sure I can anymore."

"McCABE," Mitch answered his office phone Monday afternoon in his clipped professional voice.

"Have you heard from Jackson?" Grady barked.

Normally Mitch might make a smart-ass remark just to annoy Grady, but something clicked when Grady asked about Jackson. Something wasn't right. "He's not at Lackland?"

"No," Grady answered. "And as of tonight, he'll be AWOL."

Jackson hadn't picked up his duffel last night, but Mitch had just assumed he'd spent the night with the Keno girl after they found her mother, and then gone straight to the airport from there. "Jackson would never be AWOL if he could help it."

"You know that. And I know that. Now we just have to find him."

"I'll call Hughes," Mitch said as he flipped open his

cell phone. "She took the morning off. Maybe she knows something."

"Good idea. In the meantime, I'll call Ms. Brenner. I have her number from yesterday. Jackson was still with her last I saw him."

COLE FELT as though the desert sun was boiling him alive. He'd made it to the highway, but not one car had come by in all the time he'd been walking. One painful step at a time, he limped along, holding his ribs, pretty sure something serious was wrong with his right knee. The thirst was making him lose his mind. He kept thinking he was in Iraq. Then the next minute a plane would fly overhead or he'd see a billboard.

The thought occurred to him, he could die out here and no one would know for days. At least in Iraq he'd had a crew looking for him and his approximate location after he ejected.

Why the hell had he been such a fool last night, riding so recklessly after the shots of tequila? Did he actually have a death wish? He'd rationalized his actions in Iraq with the excuse that he was saving soldiers, but what was his excuse this time?

He was lucky even to be alive. Albeit no one knew where he was. Lackland would consider him AWOL by now. They'd call his squadron commander, who might call Grady or McCabe. Damn. What if they called Jordan looking for him? She'd already spent a hellish day searching for her mother. Maybe she'd be too pissed to care where he was.

He knew better though.

She'd worry. She'd be upset.

And he didn't want that. He wished only good things for her. If only he could have been one of them. But he'd lost any chance of having something meaningful with her.

That thought hurt worse than his ribs.

And as simple as that, he knew he loved her. And he knew what he wanted. He wanted Jordan. He needed her. How could he have not known that before? Before it was too late.

Are you happy now, Jackson, you ass? What was so great about having no responsibilities? He had his "freedom," but what did that buy him? Look how shallow his life was without someone who really cared for him. Damn.

He loved Jordan. Now that he'd acknowledged that to himself, he wanted to tell her. To make things right. Right now. And mostly he wanted her in his arms.

He heard a hawk screech above him and raised his eyes to the sky. It seemed to be a symbol, and he swore to himself that as soon as he made it to civilization he'd get his shit together, sort out his life, and then do whatever it took to win Jordan back.

He pulled his shirt off, tied it around his head and pushed on. Back to Vegas. Back to Jordan.

If she'd have him.

JORDAN STROLLED around the casino, trailing her free hand across unoccupied slots. Her feet ached. Her uniform chafed. Her vision was distorted. And several customers had been forced to repeat themselves when her mind wandered. How was she going to be bright-eyed for her interview tomorrow?

The new suit would help.

And it was time for her break. She checked her phone messages first thing as usual and listened to Mrs. Simco's report on her mom, then there was a strange message from Cole.

"Jordan, need to talk to you," he said. Just hearing his voice made her pulse jump and skitter. He'd be in Texas by now.

"I wanted to do this in person, but—" His voice sounded slurred and there were some weird noises in the background. "I know now." Some more noise that sounded as if he was fumbling with the phone. "I know what I want, Jordan."

Jordan squeezed her eyes shut. He sounded drunk.

"Major Jackson!" Jordan heard some female's voice and more phone fumbling. "The doctor said you're to be resting. Oh, you're burning up." And the phone clicked off.

Doctor? Burning up? Jordan called the number on her received calls list. A woman answered, "University Medical Center." Cole was in the hospital?

She quickly ended the call and grabbed her back-pack, then headed for the time clock to punch out. The timecard was slid halfway in when she caught herself.

What was to be gained by her being there? There was nowhere for their relationship to go. Relationship? Hah. They didn't even have a relationship.

What had Cole said? She replayed the message. Her

heart squeezed when she concluded it was probably pain meds that made him sound slurred. And yet…what was the difference? He still hadn't been in his right mind. Would he have even called her if he hadn't been in such a condition?

She punched in Alex's number. Alex would know what to do and who to notify. After giving her the information, Jordan slipped her phone inside her backpack and returned to work on the casino floor.

It wasn't long before she was just going through the motions. Her mind was spinning. What had happened? Was he going to be okay? Maybe she should go to him.

She didn't wait for another break to call Alex to see if Cole was okay. Relationship or not, she had to know what was going on. If she got fired, she really couldn't have cared less.

EARLY Tuesday morning Alex banged on Mitch's apartment door.

McCabe jerked the door open wearing nothing but low-riding jeans, looking red-eyed, disheveled and hungover.

Alex bit back a smile and folded her arms. A smidgeon of satisfaction sparked at getting revenge for the other night. But it hit her that he was really worried. He truly cared for Jackson. If only he'd let that caring person out of its closely guarded prison.

"You got news?" McCabe growled.

"Jackson's in the hospital."

In an instant, Mitch's posture stiffened and his gaze became alert. "He's okay, though. Right?"

"He'll be fine."

"Well, why the hell didn't someone call?" He left her in the doorway and disappeared down the hall.

Alex followed him inside the apartment and plunked down on his couch. "Your cell must be dead. I keep telling you to get a land line."

Mitch poked his head around the corner of the hallway. "I need to shower. Come on back and fill me in while I shave." Then he disappeared into his bedroom again.

Alex froze. Then she blinked. Then she swallowed. Fine. She pushed off the sofa and sauntered down the hall to his bedroom. She could do this. He'd be in the bathroom anyway.

He was standing at his bathroom counter—in his underwear— shaving as she passed the bathroom door and sat on his bed. No big deal, Hughes. No big deal. They'd been friends for a long time.

Man, why had she never noticed how fine his butt looked in tighty whities?

"So, what happened?" he called out. Alex jumped, shocked at her thoughts. Get your mind in the game, Hughes.

"He wrecked his bike Sunday night. Out in the middle of nowhere. Walked for a while and then finally hitched a ride back to town. No major injuries. Broken ribs, concussion, a banged-up knee. But otherwise good."

"How'd you find out? My cell couldn't have been dead for long. I was still out looking for him until I came home to grab a few hours of shuteye."

"Yeah, that's the thing. The only person he called from the hospital was Jordan."

"The Keno girl?"

Alex heard the shower curtain yanked back and the water turned on. Was he naked? Argh! What was the matter with her? "Yeah, but evidently he was hopped up on medication and wasn't making much sense. Jordan got scared. She was at work and couldn't leave, so she called me."

Alex heard Mitch swear long and in great detail from behind the shower curtain. "What about his AWOL status?"

"Grady's working on it. But he says Jackson was talking crazy when he called."

The shower turned off, the curtain yanked back again. Alex bolted off the bed and paced to the window just as Mitch came out in nothing but a towel. Why was this bothering her all of a sudden? She'd seen him in his underwear before. Hell, she'd seen him in a towel before.

"What kind of crazy stuff?" Alex heard Mitch open a drawer and close it, and then the closet door opened.

"Grady said Jackson told him he was going to quit the Air Force. Said he was going to ask for a discharge."

Another long string of curse words filtered from the closet, and then Mitch walked out buttoning his uniform shirt. "He had to be out of his mind. I'll talk to him. Let's go."

"Take your own car, I have to be at work in a couple of hours."

"MAJOR Jackson?"

Cole winced and blinked his eyes open. Then shut them against the bright light.

"Major Jackson, can you hear me?" an unfamiliar male voice roared next to his ear, splitting his head into jagged pieces.

"I'm sure everyone in Nevada can hear you," Cole grumbled. His head throbbed like a son of a bitch. He raised a hand to cover his eyes, but something tugged on his arm. He opened one eye and stared at the IV attached to the back of his hand.

He dropped his hand and looked in the direction of the voice. A young African-American man in a white coat with a stethoscope around his neck stood peering at him.

Producing a penlight, the doc leaned over Cole, poked his eyelid open and fired a light into first one eye, then the other. "Pupils responding. Do you know where you are, Major?"

"In hell?"

The doc grunted. "His sense of humor's intact. I guess he can have visitors for a few minutes."

"Thank you, Doctor." That was Grady's voice. And Grady shaking the doc's hand.

Silence permeated the room for several long seconds. It was so quiet Cole could hear voices outside and down the hall.

Grady stalked to the window, and opened the blinds to a sunny Las Vegas day. "I contacted your commander at Lackland. He wants to be notified as soon as you're discharged here."

Cole cleared his throat. "Thanks." He reached for the pitcher of water on the table beside his bed and his head exploded. "Think I could get some aspirin?"

Grady stalked over to Cole and poured him some water as McCabe strode in, with Hughes right behind him.

"You know, Jackson, if you've got a thing for nurses, there are easier ways to get their attention." McCabe flashed a huge grin and wiggled his brows.

Cole smiled, glad to see his friends. "McCabe, you dog. I was just telling Grady, here, that I'm fine. You can't keep using me as an excuse to get out of work." His grin faded and his gaze shifted to Hughes, who was standing behind McCabe. "Did you talk to her?"

Hughes stepped forward, shaking her head. "She has a job interview this morning. Give her some time."

"Oh, yeah, I remember her saying—"

"Come on, Jackson," McCabe scoffed. "You aren't seriously thinking about getting out?"

Cole nodded. "As soon as I report to Lackland I'm going to request a discharge."

"Jackson, think about what you're doing." McCabe's voice was strained. "You've got twelve years of service. How bad can controlling air traffic in Texas be?"

"That's not it. I've been thinking a lot lately about what I want to do with my life. And I need to be out there. On the front line, making a difference."

"What are you planning?" Hughes studied him, her eyes narrowed.

Cole grinned and spread his arms wide. "What else? Las Vegas P.D."

While Grady raised his brows, and Hughes nodded her approval, McCabe's jaw dropped. "Police? You want to be a cop?"

"If they'll have me. I'll have to pass the tests, and the physicals, but...yeah." And as soon as he started that ball rolling, he'd move on to his next mission: win back a woman's love and then spend the rest of his life loving her.

Jordan. He missed the sound of her voice, her touch, her smile.

There were inherent risks involved in his plan, but the thrill buzzing around inside him told him he'd begun a new adventure. The quest of a lifetime. Winning Jordan back would be the biggest challenge of his life. Cole smiled. He did love a good challenge.

14

IT WAS her first day at her new job. And Jordan loved the work. She had a salaried position she'd dreamed of for years. Her own cubicle. Some nice coworkers. And last week, she'd had a heartfelt goodbye party at The Grand where everyone had chipped in to buy her a gift card to her favorite department store.

But when a florist delivered an arrangement of red and yellow roses to her cubicle that morning, Jordan's heart soared. She knew what that particular combination of colors meant. And she knew only one other person with that knowledge.

Cole.

Two weeks. Two weeks since she'd last seen him.

In two weeks her life had completely changed. She'd been offered the position with Nevada Power and had accepted it. The building where she worked was downtown, within blocks of a bus stop. She'd given notice at The Grand and found a well-run adult day-care facility for her mother. And now she worked days and had weekends off like a regular person.

So how did Cole know where she worked?

Alex.

She fished a five-dollar bill out of her wallet and stuffed it into the deliveryman's hand, hardly waiting until he left before snatching the card from its plastic holder.

I never stop thinking of you
C

Jordan drew in a long slow breath. Why did he have to reopen the wound? There was no point. That chapter of her life was closed.

"Beautiful roses."

Jordan looked up and realized she'd been staring at the card while holding her breath. "Too beautiful not to share," she said as she picked up the vase. Without giving herself a chance to think twice, she carried the bouquet to the break room and set them on the table. Out of her sight.

But Cole was never really out of her thoughts.

She could keep herself busy in her waking hours. Yet when she slept, that's when he invaded her mind. When she dreamed, it was of Cole.

Cole, handing her a bag with a carton of Ben and Jerry's ice cream. Cole, playing cards with her mom. Cole on his motorcycle, his shirt open to her touch...

The next day at work, Jordan was just about to open her brown-bag lunch when a man appeared at her cubicle wearing a chef's apron and hat. He carried a silver tray with a chrome-covered plate. "Ms. Brenner?"

Jordan blinked up at the man. "Yes?"

"Compliments of a Major Jackson." He set the tray on her desk and whipped off the cover. The chef had attracted a crowd of her coworkers and several people oohed and awwed. Sautéed shrimp with prosciutto. Pasta and asparagus steaming with flavor. It was the same meal Cole had made for her the night of her graduation.

"Th-thank you," she finally stuttered.

The chef bowed, and left.

The tray held a slim vase with a single red rose, a thick napkin, silverware, iced tea in a crystal glass, but...

"Wait!" She jumped up and chased after the chef.

He stopped and turned.

"Was there a note or a message?"

"No, ma'am. Just that it was with his compliments."

"Oh." Jordan's shoulders sagged. "Thank you again."

By the time she made it back to her cubicle, the crowd had grown and everyone was staring at her. "I'm so sorry for the disruption." Her first week at work and what an impression she must be making.

"Are you kidding?" one lady answered for the crowd. "This is the most exciting thing to happen around here in forever."

"Aren't you going to eat that?" another lady asked.

"Yeah, don't let it get cold," chimed in the guy who worked across the aisle from her.

Jordan nodded and picked up her fork as everyone wandered away. The meal sure beat a bologna sandwich. The flavors of garlic and cream, several cheeses and shrimp melted together and exploded on her tongue.

What was she supposed to glean from this? Was she supposed to call Cole and thank him? Shouldn't she? That was what he wanted.

Could she?

Once she heard his voice her resolve for a clean break would dissolve. All the pain of the past weeks would be for nothing.

Wasn't it already?

She'd never be able to go back to the clear-cut and simple life she'd lived a couple of months ago. Everything had been black and white then. School: good. Getting swept off her feet: bad.

Now there were shades of gray.

She loved him.

On Wednesday, the largest box of Godiva chocolates Jordan had ever seen, gold-leafed, embossed and heart-shaped, was delivered to her desk. This time there was a note, but the usual crowd of coworkers lingered until she opened the box and offered a piece to everyone.

As soon as the group dissipated, Jordan slipped the sealed note in her purse and headed for the ladies' room.

Her fingers trembled as she peeled open the envelope and pulled out the card.

Did you get the meal from Delmonico's?
I miss you
C

Cole. She could smell him. Feel him. Hear him.
What was she going to do? This had to stop. Where

was the peace and acceptance she needed to move on? But how could she move on, when he wouldn't let her?

She ducked into a stall and pressed her palms into her eyes. You're an idiot, Jordan Brenner. It was a waste of time feeling sorry for oneself. Trust that you made the right decision, stop letting him sway you, and move on.

Looking down at her palms, she noticed she'd smeared her mascara. Great. She pulled out some tissues and repaired her face as best she could.

On Thursday, he went too far. "Okay, now, *this* has just got to stop." Jordan fisted her hands on her hips and stared in disbelief.

The security guard had called her down to the lobby of the company's high rise building to sign for a delivery. When she stepped out of the elevator, a man was waiting to hand her a key.

Jordan walked outside and there in the circular drive sat a brand-new, bright-sunshine-yellow Volkswagen Beetle with a huge red ribbon around it and bow on the roof.

The deliveryman holding a clipboard with papers to sign moved to stand beside her. "Jordan Brenner?"

At her nod, he held out a note. "Here's a message for you."

There was no way Jordan could accept the car, but she snatched the note from his hand.

I didn't choose the convertible
See how responsible I've become?
C

Jordan burst into a laugh, and then held her fingers over her lips as it turned into a cry. She turned to the man with the clipboard. "I can't sign for this. You'll have to take it back."

The man blinked. "You don't want it?"

Jordan shook her head as she crossed the street to a park. Cole had to quit doing these things. She sat on a bench, pulled out her cell phone and punched in Alex's number.

"Major Hughes," Alex answered.

"Is he crazy? I can't accept a car."

"I tried to tell him."

"Well, he should have listened to you."

"Jordan." Alex sighed. "Just call him."

"Why doesn't he call me?" Jordan cringed to hear how petty that sounded.

"He thinks you won't listen to what he has to say. And, for what it's worth, you should. What can it hurt?"

"I don't know."

"Do you love him?"

Jordan paused. "Loving someone and trusting them always to be there for you are two different things."

There was silence on the other end of the line, and then Alex said, "True. I can't argue with that. Talk later."

"Yeah," Jordan managed the one syllable past the lump in her throat, and then snapped her phone shut.

OKAY. So, maybe she missed his daily gifts.

After a week of not hearing from Cole, Jordan seemed to go through the five stages of grief like a textbook patient.

First there was denial. She didn't care. It was a good thing. She *wanted* to be left alone so she could move on with her life. And she suited action to feelings. After spending the morning at the coin laundry Saturday, Jordan took her mom to the nail salon and celebrated her new salary by getting them both a manicure and pedicure. She couldn't care less about Cole Jackson.

Second was anger. How dare he send her all those romantic gifts? And the notes? What kind of mind game was he playing? Did he understand that he had gotten her hopes up?

After taking her mom to church Sunday morning, Jordan spent the afternoon cleaning her apartment from top to bottom, scrubbing extra hard and extra long just for good measure.

The third stage was bargaining. Maybe she should have called him. Or at least sent a thank-you note. If she called him now, maybe it wouldn't be too late.

On Monday, at work, Jordan picked up her cell phone and almost called Cole a dozen times during the day. In addition, she composed an e-mail thanking him, but she never hit Send. She even started to buy an online greeting card with a corny thank-you message. But at the last minute she canceled it.

This led to the fourth stage of grief: Depression. Of course it was too late. It had always been too late. Their situation was hopeless. How could she have ever believed anything else? Even if she were willing to trust in a long-distance relationship, he'd obviously moved on when she didn't respond. He got the message. She should be happy. Wasn't that what she wanted?

On Wednesday night she stopped by the store after work, bought a half gallon of double chocolate chunk ice cream and ate it straight out of the carton while her mom watched television.

And at last, the final stage: Acceptance. Thursday morning, a sense of peace hit Jordan as she sat at her desk at work and opened up her e-mail. She accepted that Cole had moved on. That was what she'd needed. And that was why she hadn't responded to his gifts. This was a good thing. Eventually she'd be able to look back on this experience with gratitude for what it had taught her.

15

"I CAN'T BELIEVE you did it, man." McCabe thunked three beers and a glass of water on the table and then sat across from Cole in a booth at a pool hall close to Nellis.

"Believe it." Cole grabbed one of the beers and sipped. "I'm out."

As of yesterday, Cole was no longer officially an Air Force man. The moment Cole signed his honorable discharge papers he'd felt the weight of an F-22 lift off his chest. He'd loved the Air Force and all the opportunities it had provided him. He'd loved serving his country and even the job as an air traffic controller wouldn't have been half bad. More money than he'd see as a cop, that was for sure.

But there was more to life than money.

"And, it gets worse," Cole sipped his beer and shot Hughes a conspiratorial grin.

"What?" McCabe looked back and forth between Hughes and Cole. "What have you gone and done now?"

Hughes gestured with her beer. "Look out the window."

McCabe stretched his neck to look. "Aw, jeez, Jackson. A sedan? You loved riding that hog."

"Yeah, but it's kind of hard to take two special ladies out on it."

"Two?"

Hughes cleared her throat. "Jordan and her mom, hello?"

Cole smiled at Hughes. "Where's Grady?"

"Right here." Grady slid in next to Cole. "Good to see you out of the hospital, Jackson."

"Thanks."

"So, you're going to be a cop, huh?"

Cole was anxious to start at the police academy. It had felt right the minute he'd applied to the Las Vegas police force. He was looking forward to it, maybe he could do some good.

He still had to go through police training, but he'd passed all the tests and they seemed eager to have ex-military personnel on the force. Even ones who were deaf in one ear. "Yeah, they might let me write tickets and everything," he answered Grady. "And no favors. You guys break the speed limit, I'm writing your ass a ticket."

"That's kind of like letting a jewel thief guard the crown jewels, isn't it?" Grady's lip curled, the closest he ever got to smiling.

"Joke all you want," Cole said. "But I get a pair of handcuffs."

"Hey, I never thought of that," McCabe said, and Hughes rammed her elbow into his ribs.

"Don't encourage him, Jackson. Ever since his thirty days were up, he's been worse than ever," warned Hughes.

Grady raised a brow. "Did you expect him to take to celibacy?"

"Guess we can't call him Monk Man anymore, huh?" Cole chortled.

"Hell, no." McCabe rubbed his hands together. "McCabe the Babe Magnet is back."

Hughes shook her head at him then turned her attention to Cole. "So, what are you going to do about Jordan?"

"I have a few aces left up my sleeve."

Jordan hadn't called him. Hadn't written. No response to his gifts. Well, fine. She'd been a challenge for him from the day he'd met her, and he hadn't given up then. She wanted to play hard to win? It was time to step up the game.

"Have you thought about simply calling her and telling her you love her?"

"Aw, man, now why would he want to do that?"

Cole ignored McCabe. "I could." He'd thought about it. "But where's the challenge?" Besides, he wasn't sure he could take it if she said nothing and hung up.

And there was one other reason. He wanted her to meet him halfway. He had to know she wanted him enough to take him as he was.

In the meantime, placing an online order at Ben and Jerry's was a good start.

"Hey, I just thought of something." McCabe slowly smiled. A huge grin combined with an evil glint in his eye.

"I don't like that look," Hughes narrowed her eyes at McCabe. "Can we get him to lose another bet?"

"Hughes, you know me too well. But it's Grady's

turn. He never went for that massage. And now that Jackson is back in town…"

"Name the day." Grady swallowed his ice water.

Cole found it fitting that's all he ever drank. Ice water probably ran through Grady's veins.

THAT EVENING on the other side of town, Jordan was just leaving work for the day when her cell phone rang.

"Hey, it's Alex, you want to grab some din—"

"What's happened to Cole? Has he hurt himself again? Why haven't I heard from him?" As Sherri would have said: acceptance schmeptance.

"Whoa. Calm down," Alex soothed. "Jackson is healthy as a horse."

"Then why hasn't he—"

"Jordan. Stop. I can't be your go-between. If you want to know what's going on with Jackson, call him yourself." Jordan heard her mutter something about who was more stubborn.

Jordan closed her eyes, tried to picture herself calling Cole. She took a deep breath and exhaled. "You're right. I'm sorry. You wanted to meet for supper?"

There was a moment of silence on the other end of the line. Then Alex said, "Yeah, it's ladies' night at McGully's."

At happy hour with Alex, Jordan downed her weight's worth of chips and salsa and guzzled a half-price margarita before leaving to pick up her mom from the adult day care. Mom had had a good day today, and Jordan put on a DVD she rented for the evening. After tucking her mother into bed, Jordan sat beside her and smoothed her hair, humming an old tune from her childhood.

"Jordie?" her mom spoke without opening her eyes.

"What is it, Mama?"

"Brush your teeth."

Jordan smiled and rubbed her mom's arm. "I will, Mama."

Her mother had always been there to listen when Jordan needed to talk out her problems. She wanted to lie down beside her mom and be a kid again. Let her mom tell her what to do. "What should I do, Mama?"

Jordan moved to the chair beside the bed and rocked in the darkness. "I know. You think since I can't stop thinking about him, I should call him.

"But I can't call him because—" she rocked harder as she dug deep to find the truth "—because I'm too scared."

In her imagination, her mama asked what was she scared of.

"I'm afraid of—" And the rocker creaked as Jordan thought about the real reason. "I'm afraid because I love him so much, I wouldn't recover if he left me like Ian did."

In her mind, her mother smiled and said, "Oh, honey, you can never have true joy living in fear. You're miserable now. And you're strong enough to recover from anything, believe me."

Jordan rocked some more and thought about it. She had survived being abandoned before. Was happiness with Cole worth risking the pain? Could she give him her trust? It might mean picking up and moving to wherever he got stationed, with no guarantee if it didn't work out.

She promised herself she wouldn't move until her mother was settled in a full-time facility. Her doctors had assured Jordan that Tammy would require that within the next year. She'd have to make do with a long-distance relationship with Cole until then.

And this was assuming Cole still wanted something with her.

But she wanted to try. Just deciding that made a gurgle of happiness bubble up inside her. She shot out of the rocker and bent to kiss her mother's cheek. "Thank you for listening, Mama," she whispered to her.

Before she could stop herself she went in the living room, found the number on her cell, and hit the call button. After a couple of rings, she got a recording that the number had been disconnected and was no longer in service.

THE MORNING was busy at work and Jordan didn't manage to get Cole's new number from Alex until late afternoon. Better not to call him until after work anyway. She needed privacy for this conversation.

At the end of the day, Jordan closed down her computer, gathered up her briefcase and purse, and headed for the elevator. Once she got to the lobby, her hands shook so badly, she tried twice before she punched the correct numbers on her cell.

Heat blasted her as soon as she stepped out of the revolving doors. She took a deep breath and punched the call button. After two rings, her stomach was churning, she felt nauseous.

"Jackson," he answered.

Jordan tried to breath slowly. Cole's deep voice seemed to vibrate all through her.

"Hello? Jordan?"

"Yeah, I'm here." She came to a corner and stood in a crowd of commuters waiting for the traffic. "I wondered if maybe we could talk."

A heartbeat of silence, then "We can."

"I—I've been thinking. If, if you still wanted—"

"I still want."

"Oh. Um…" She was going about this all wrong. She should have thanked him for the flowers and the meal and asked about his injuries. Why hadn't she prepared something?

"You still there?"

"I'm here. And I want to try to make things work with you. Maybe I could come to San Antonio some weekend? I found a great place for my mom during the day. She really likes it. And we could see how it goes."

"Jordan. Where are you?"

She checked her surroundings. "I'm downtown. There's a bus stop about three blocks from my office building. I'm almost there. Why? Is the traffic too noisy? Can you hear me okay?"

"Do me a favor?"

"Uh, sure."

"Don't take the first bus that comes along."

Jordan blinked as she crossed the street with other pedestrians. Was that supposed to be a metaphor? "Cole. I know what I want. And it's you. I should have told you that the night you found my mom. I love you. I want you. I want us to be together some day."

"I want that, too. But, just don't get on that bus, okay?"

What was he trying to say? "Cole. I'm saying I know I shouldn't be afraid anymore. I know I need to trust you. You taught me sometimes in life we have to take a risk."

"And you've taught me that sometimes the most exciting adventures happen when you take on a couple of responsibilities."

For the first time in weeks, Jordan smiled all the way from her eyes to her toes. "Really?" She was almost to the bus stop and a bus was just gasping away. "The bus just left without me."

"I know."

"What do you mean? How could you—?"

"Turn around."

Jordan spun on her heels and scanned the parking lot behind her. A tall, dark man straightened from where he'd been leaning against a midnight-blue sedan. He had his elbow bent, his hand to his ear.

"Like my new car?" He took his other hand out of his pocket and began walking toward her.

She couldn't breathe. Or she was breathing too much. She couldn't believe he was here. It was like déjà vu, but not.

"What are you doing here?" She dropped the phone to her side as he got closer. The breadth and width of him, the heat and nearness of his body. His hair was cut short, and his jaw was dark with stubble. He had the same penetrating gaze, his dark brown eyes radiating heat.

He reached out to touch her cheek and a razor-edged zing shot through her body. She gulped in air and his unique scent permeated her senses. Musky cologne, leather…Cole. Goose bumps rose on her arms and the back of her neck.

Beneath his starched, muted-green dress shirt his chest rose and fell and he set his jaw. "I love you, Jordan Brenner." He pulled her into his arms, dipped his head and took her mouth.

Jordan forgot about catching the bus, wrapped her arms around his neck and leaned in for his kiss.

Epilogue

COLE STOOD from the dinner table and reached for his belt. He checked his gun, holstered it, then checked his radio. He'd been accepted on the Las Vegas police force a month ago, and he loved it.

"I finally get a day job and now you work nights." Jordan came in from the kitchen and put her arms around him from behind. She waited until after he left for work in the evenings to pick her mom up from the adult day-care facility. It gave them a little time alone.

Cole took Tammy "to see her friends" in the mornings when he got off his shift—usually after they played a mean game of Gin. It might not be the ideal situation, but it worked for them. For now.

"We'll have the weekend, babe." Cole reached for his bullet-proof vest, but Jordan grabbed his hand.

"Don't put that on yet." She sighed and rested her cheek between his shoulder blades and nuzzled into his back. "Remember when I used to ride behind you on your motorcycle?" She slid one hand beneath his belt and cupped him over his zipper with the other.

Cole groaned as his cock hardened. "You keep that

up, I'll be late for my shift." Jordan had only been home for half an hour. This schedule sure was counterproductive to his love life.

"So, take a risk. Be late." Still nuzzling along his spine, she unzipped his uniform pants.

He grabbed her hand, spun around and clasped her waist. "Did I ever tell you—" walking her backward into the kitchen, he lifted her up onto the kitchen counter and reached beneath her T-shirt to pull it over her head "—I like the way you think?" She was naked beneath the shirt and he almost lost control as he stepped between her thighs and ran his hands over her soft skin, cupping her breasts.

"Stop talking and kiss me." Jordan covered his mouth with a deep, sensual kiss, stabbing her fingers through his hair.

Cole made quick work of shedding his belt with all its equipment. It dropped with a thud to the floor.

"Hey," Jordan protested as she gave him room to finish unzipping his pants. "We might need those handcuffs."

Cole stilled with his mouth halfway to her nipple as images formed of Jordan handcuffed to their bed. "Baby, don't make promises you can't keep."

"I was talking about using them on you," she whispered as she took his stiff cock in her hand and stroked down the length of him.

"Hmm." That would never happen. Although no sense in spoiling her dream right now. He suckled hard on her nipple and tested her readiness. "Jordan. You keep playing with that and I won't be able to go slow."

"So arrest me, Mr. Policeman." She scooted forward and fitted him to her. "I have a need."

Raising his head to catch her eye, he couldn't stop a smile. "Don't say it, Brenner." A guttural sound escaped his throat as he pushed inside her and he closed his eyes as her tight warmth surrounded him.

Jordan locked her ankles behind his back and moved her hips against him. "Come on." She grinned up at him, her blue eyes sparkling with mischief. "I want to say it." She nibbled little kisses along his jaw and down his neck. "Please?"

He tangled his fingers in her hair and brought her mouth to his. "No," he mumbled against her lips, pulled his cock out slowly and pushed back in just as slow.

"Cole," she groaned his name in two syllables. "I *need* to say it. That's why they call this a quickie."

He felt her smile beneath his lips, but he deepened the kiss, moving his tongue in to taste her. Damn, he loved playing this game with her. Hell, he just plain loved her. "No."

She made a sweet mewling sound as he tortured her with slow, steady strokes, caressing her spine with one hand, her breast with the other. "How are you gonna stop me, Officer?"

"Like this." He moved his hand down to tease her clit with his thumb.

Throwing her head back, she moaned long and breathy, wiggling her hips even faster. "Ooh, Officer Jackson, that's good."

It was killing him trying to keep his pace slow. "Trust

me, ma'am." He pumped a little faster, biting gently on her shoulder. "I know what's best for you."

"Cole?" She slid her hand down between them to play with his chest. Twirling a finger in his chest hair and tweaking his nipple.

"Yeah?" Helpless to stop himself, he thrust hard, setting a faster pace.

"I think you feel the need, too."

He grunted. "Brenner…" Her name was spoken as part warning, part plea.

She laughed out loud and then groaned her encouragement as he drove home, grabbing her butt, thrusting faster. "The need for—ahh…" She came hard and stiffened in his arms.

Just watching the pleasure take over her body drove Cole over the edge. One last thrust took him to heaven, safe in her arms, wrapped in her love.

* * * * *

*In honor of our 60th anniversary,
Harlequin® American Romance® is celebrating
by featuring an all-American male each month,
all year long with*
MEN MADE IN AMERICA!
*This June, we'll be featuring American men
living in the West.*

Here's a sneak preview of
THE CHIEF RANGER *by Rebecca Winters.*

*Chief Ranger Vance Rossiter has to confront the sister
of a man who died while under Vance's watch...and
also confront his attraction to her.*

"Chief Ranger Rossiter?" The sight of the woman who'd stepped inside Vance's office brought him to his feet. "I'm Rachel Darrow. Your secretary said I should come right in."

"Please," he said, walking around his desk to shake her hand. At a glance he estimated she was in her mid-twenties. Her feminine curves did wonders for the pale blue T-shirt and jeans she was wearing. "Ranger Jarvis informed me there's a young boy with you."

The unfriendly expression in her beautiful green eyes caught him off guard. "Yes," was her clipped reply. "When we arrived in Yosemite the ranger told me I couldn't go anywhere in the park until I talked to you first."

"That's right."

"Knowing you wanted this meeting to be private, he offered to show my nephew around Headquarters."

So this woman was the victim's sister.... "What's his name?"

"Nicky."

The boy who haunted Vance's dreams now had a name. "How old is he?"

"He turned six three weeks ago. Were you the man in charge when my brother and sister-in-law were killed?"

"Yes. To tell you I'm sorry for what happened couldn't begin to convey my feelings."

The woman's gaze didn't flicker. "I won't even try to describe mine. Just tell me one thing. Was their accident preventable?"

"Yes," he answered without hesitation.

"In other words, the people working under you fell asleep on your watch and two lives were snuffed out as a result."

Hearing it put like that, he had to set the record straight. "My staff had nothing to do with it. I, myself, could have prevented the loss of life."

Ms. Darrow's expression hardened. "So you admit culpability."

"Yes. I take full blame."

A look of pain crossed over her features. "You can just stand there and admit it?" Her cry echoed that of his own tortured soul.

"Yes." He sucked in his breath.

"I work for a cruise line. Aboard ship, it's the captain's responsibility to maintain rigid safety regulations. If a disaster like that had happened while he was in charge he would have been relieved of his command and never given another ship again."

Rachel Darrow couldn't know she was preaching to the converted. "If you've come to the park with the intention of bringing a lawsuit against me for negligence, maybe you should." It would only be what he deserved.

"Maybe I will."

In the next instant, she wheeled around and hurried out of his office. Vance could have gone after her, but it would cause a scene, something he was loath to do for a variety of reasons. In the first place, he needed to cool down before he approached her again.

The discovery of the Darrows' frozen bodies had affected every ranger in the park. A little boy had been orphaned—a boy whose aunt was all he had left.

* * * * *

Will Rachel allow Vance to explain—
and will she let him into her heart?
Find out in
THE CHIEF RANGER
Available June 2009 from
Harlequin® American Romance®.

We'll be spotlighting a different series every month
throughout 2009 to celebrate our 60th anniversary.

Look for Harlequin®
American Romance® in June!

Join us for a year-long celebration of the rugged
American male! From cops to cowboys—
Men Made in America has the hero
you've been dreaming about!

Look for

The Chief Ranger

by Rebecca Winters, on sale in June!

Bachelor CEO by Michele Dunaway	July
The Rodeo Rider by Roxann Delaney	August
Doctor Daddy by Jacqueline Diamond	September

nocturne™

New York Times Bestselling Author

REBECCA BRANDEWYNE

FROM THE MISTS OF WOLF CREEK

Hallie Muldoon suspects that her grandmother
has special abilities, but her sudden death
forces Hallie to return to Wolf Creek, where
details emerge of a spell cast. Local farmer
Trace Coltrane and the wolf that prowls around
the farmhouse both appear out of nowhere, and
a killer has Hallie in his sights. With no other
choice, Hallie relies on Trace for help,
not knowing if the mysterious Trace is a
mesmerizing friend or a deadly foe....

Available June wherever books are sold.

REQUEST YOUR FREE BOOKS!

2 FREE NOVELS PLUS 2 FREE GIFTS!

HARLEQUIN®

Blaze™

Red-hot reads!

YES! Please send me 2 FREE Harlequin® Blaze™ novels and my 2 FREE gifts (gifts are worth about $10). After receiving them, if I don't wish to receive any more books, I can return the shipping statement marked "cancel". If I don't cancel, I will receive 6 brand-new novels every month and be billed just $4.24 per book in the U.S. or $4.71 per book in Canada. Shipping and handling is just 25¢ per book. That's a savings of 15% or more off the cover price! I understand that accepting the 2 free books and gifts places me under no obligation to buy anything. I can always return a shipment and cancel at any time. Even if I never buy another book, the two free books and gifts are mine to keep forever.

151 HDN ERVA   351 HDN ERUX

Name	(PLEASE PRINT)

Address	Apt. #

City	State/Prov.	Zip/Postal Code

Signature (if under 18, a parent or guardian must sign)

Mail to the **Harlequin Reader Service:**
IN U.S.A.: P.O. Box 1867, Buffalo, NY 14240-1867
IN CANADA: P.O. Box 609, Fort Erie, Ontario L2A 5X3

Not valid to current subscribers of Harlequin Blaze books.

Want to try two free books from another line?
Call 1-800-873-8635 or visit www.morefreebooks.com.

* Terms and prices subject to change without notice. Prices do not include applicable taxes. N.Y. residents add applicable sales tax. Canadian residents will be charged applicable provincial taxes and GST. Offer not valid in Quebec. This offer is limited to one order per household. All orders subject to approval. Credit or debit balances in a customer's account(s) may be offset by any other outstanding balance owed by or to the customer. Please allow 4 to 6 weeks for delivery. Offer available while quantities last.

Your Privacy: Harlequin Books is committed to protecting your privacy. Our Privacy Policy is available online at www.eHarlequin.com or upon request from the Reader Service. From time to time we make our lists of customers available to reputable third parties who may have a product or service of interest to you. If you would prefer we not share your name and address, please check here. ☐

HB09R

You're invited to join our Tell Harlequin Reader Panel!

By joining our new reader panel you will:

- Receive Harlequin® books—they are FREE and yours to keep with no obligation to purchase anything!
- Participate in fun online surveys
- Exchange opinions and ideas with women just like you
- Have a say in our new book ideas and help us publish the best in women's fiction

In addition, you will have a chance to win great prizes and receive special gifts! See Web site for details. Some conditions apply. Space is limited.

To join, visit us at
www.TellHarlequin.com.

THBPA0108

COMING NEXT MONTH

Available May 26, 2009

#471 BRANDED Tori Carrington
Jo Atchison isn't your average cowgirl. She's rough, she's tough and she's sexy as hell. And regardless of the rules, she wants rancher Trace Armstrong. Luckily, Trace wants Jo, too. The only one not happy about it is Jo's volatile boyfriend....

#472 WHEN THE SUN GOES DOWN... Crystal Green
A trip to Japan on family business is just the chance Juliana Thompsen and Tristan Cole have been waiting for. They've been hopelessly in love with each other for years, but a family feud made a relationship impossible. Now they're alone, and they're going to experience *everything* they've missed. But will it be enough to last them a lifetime?

#473 UNDRESSED Heather MacAllister
Encounters
Take some naughty talk, add one *very* thin wall between the last dressing room in a bridal shop and a tuxedo boutique, and what do you have? The recipe for a happy marriage...and four very satisfied—and enlightened—couples. When you get this kind of tailoring, who needs a honeymoon?

#474 TWIN TEMPTATION Cara Summers
The Wrong Bed: Again and Again
Maddie Farrell has just learned she has a twin sister. And she's an heiress. *And* she's just had sex with the hot stranger in her bed! It must be a mistake. Right? Hmm—she might have to have more sex just to make sure....

#475 LETTERS FROM HOME Rhonda Nelson
Uniformly Hot!
Ranger Levi McPherson is getting some anonymous, red-hot love letters during his tour of duty! When he comes home on leave, he's determined to track down the mysterious author...and show her that actions speak louder than words.

#476 THE MIGHTY QUINNS: BRODY Kate Hoffmann
Quinns Down Under
Runaway bride Payton Harwell thinks she's hit rock bottom when she ends up in jail—in Australia! But then sexy rebel Brody Quinn bails her out and lets her into his home, his bed, his life. Only, Payton's past isn't as far away as she thinks it is....

HBCNMBPA0509